Michael Daly was born in Rathcormac, Ireland in the 1950s and came to Britain to join the RAF at the age of seventeen.

After a successful career in the RAF Regiment, he left as a Squadron Leader and pursued a second career as a university bursar in Durham for Teikyo University of Japan, where he works to this day.

He has written fiction as a hobby for many years, but this is his first published work.

In 1985, he was awarded an MBE for military service and in 2016 the Freedom of the City of London.

He lives alone in Durham city.

Rosie (RIP)
Eric and B
Bob and Annie
Wendy and Avril

Michael Daly

THE MIDNIGHT MANNEQUINS AND OTHER STORIES

AUSTIN MACAULEY PUBLISHERS™

LONDON • CAMBRIDGE • NEW YORK • SHARJAH

A CIP catalogue record for this title is available from the British Library.

ISBN 9781398410398 (Paperback)
ISBN 9781398410404 (Hardback)
ISBN 9781398410411 (ePub e-book)

www.austinmacauley.com

First Published 2022
Austin Macauley Publishers Ltd®
1 Canada Square
Canary Wharf
London
E14 5AA

Table of Contents

Youth   9

The Midnight Mannequins   14

How Is Your Mother?   25

Jolly Good Show   33

The Price Tag   41

Love Letter   50

Lunch Without Laughter   62

The Book Club   72

Bed 7   80

The Tea Dancers   89

A Defaced Fiver   97

The Dance Band   112

Youth

Ricardo gazed at his reflection, longer than was necessary in the magnified shaving mirror, still smeared with his mother's ruby red lipstick. He arched his jet-black eyebrow and winked at his fine dark features. His father, whom he had never met, was from Sicily, but fortunately Ricardo inherited his chiselled good looks.

He splashed ample aftershave on his long neck and rushed downstairs to accept a strong coffee from his bleary-eyed mother. She stood tall and thin by the grimy gas cooker and yawned with a scary intensity. He knew from the zig-zag lipstick patterns that a man lay in her bed again; her pained expression said it all.

"Morning, Ric, you look great, son," and she yawned while adjusting her dressing gown collar.

"Morning, Mum," he said. "Thanks, I need to look my best and Christmas Eve sales depend upon it. In fact, our jobs right now rely heavily upon selling the over-priced shit!"

"You can sell anything, Ric. You have your father's good looks. He would be so proud that, his only son worked on the Kings Road, selling cosmetics," and she began to ruffle her dyed blond hair, cut with a severity that aged her.

"Well, they are not exactly cosmetics, Mum. They actually reverse the ageing process," and he mimicked the last sentence in a loud, posh voice.

She chuckled and poured herself a black coffee. "I did try your creams last month, Ric. They don't make a blind bit of difference to my increasing wrinkles."

"Sorry, Mum. Of course, I know that, but I enjoy persuading our clients that they have lost years. Sometimes, it takes a mere five minutes!" And he laughed as he grabbed an expensive-looking, leather bomber jacket with an off-white fleece collar. He turned and kissed her lightly on a flushed cheek before rushing off to Kilburn tube station.

Ricardo emerged from the Sloane Square underground into bright winter sunlight. He walked briskly past the elegantly dressed windows of Peter Jones and then stopped suddenly, to make slight adjustments to his gelled black hair. The large shop window became his stage and the sun acted as a spotlight. He preened himself and thought of fame and fortune. The staff of the 'Elixir of Youth Clinic' often complimented him on his acting ability; he was, after all only twenty-five years old and already their star salesman. Shortly after ten am, Ricardo and his new apprentice, Max, stood on the pavement with pockets full of anti-ageing samples: all cleverly packaged. "Let's rob the rich bastards for Christmas Eve," he had shouted to the others in the smart clinic, moments earlier. Ricardo had taught Max how to smile and more powerfully engage both sexes. He was told to show as much interest in the men, as in the women.

Within an hour, they had ushered six clients into the clinic: four elegant women and two very well-dressed middle-aged men.

"Well done, Max. This promises to be a bumper Christmas Eve. We fish and they gut!" said a beaming Ricardo, looking back into the busy clinic.

"I just did as you asked, Ricardo. I quickly scanned their clothes, shoes, jewellery and any evidence of designer brand shopping bags." Max nodded. "You are a pure genius."

"Thanks, mate. Still, we now need all six to purchase the crap inside," and he chuckled while preparing to disarm the wealthy looking gentleman, energetically approaching in the frosty air. Max swiftly told him that Dean would assist him, because Ricardo needed to personally attend to their latest client.

Ricardo gently took the man's arm. "Please take that seat by the side mirror, sir. Do give me your coat and scarf."

The man sat in the chair. "This must not take long, as I still have many presents to buy," and he remained stiffly upright in the worn leather chair.

"Do look up, sir." Ricardo expertly swabbed the man's left eye area with a lotion that contained caffeine. "You have very puffy eyes for your age, sir. You can't be much more than fifty," he said slyly.

"How very kind. I am well over sixty, I'm afraid," and he tried to examine his eyes in the illuminated mirror.

"Naughty! Not yet, sir. Give it a few more minutes to properly impregnate and you will be amazed at what's happened." Ricardo began to open the top drawer that instantly revealed beautifully packaged boxes of their products.

"I don't have much time you know," said the man. "You told me it would only take a minute." He moved uneasily in the chair.

"You only have one set of eyes, sir. You really must take better care of their surrounding skin surface." He lightly dabbed under the gentleman's treated eye. "Now look at your left eye, compared to the right one," and the mirror glinted in full view of his promising customer.

"Can't say I see any real difference, to be frank," said the gentleman with some disappointment.

"The change is quite extraordinary, sir. Take a closer look. Your left eye looks ten years younger than the right one." He pointed to amplify his observation.

"I have never seen anyone shed years from their face faster than you, sir."

"I'm afraid I don't agree with you, and I need to be off now," but a playful push from Ricardo made him sink back into the comfortable chair.

"Look up, sir." Even before he could reply, Ricardo was vigorously applying the cream to his right eye area. "We simply cannot have you Christmas shopping with a young and an old eye!"

He proffered the mirror at speed and regarded the gentleman's glare, uneasily. After months of selling these products that, offered little hope of regaining any lost youth, he knew from the stranger's facial expression that, all hope of a meaningful sale had already evaporated.

"You have lost twenty years already, sir." But Ricardo's voice lacked that initial 'hard sell' confidence.

"Absolute crap," said the gentleman and he swiped the mirror to one side. "If I sit here for much longer, I will lose two hundred pounds rather than years young man."

Ricardo hurriedly picked up the coffee stained, oily swabs of cotton wool and stood to one side. His unsmiling sales colleague went forward as if ready to open the door.

The gentleman took a further angry look in the large side mirror and laughed. "What made you fools think that I wanted to look younger for God's sake? I'm well over sixty and happy with my furrows and wrinkles, thank you very much."

The door banged and Ricardo took out his mobile, pretending to send a text. He knew from the gentleman's reaction that Christmas Eve was going to be rough. His tough, no nonsense American manager was already unimpressed with their branch's sales figures. Ricardo took a deep breath, smiled, and walked out on to a busy, cold Kings Road. His next sale would help to buy a nice Christmas present for his mother. Within minutes, a very rotund lady approached, laden with designer shopping bags. Perfect, he muttered while removing a shiny black sachet from his pocket.

"May I take up just one moment of your time, Madam, please?" He beamed and then he tried to hand her the little sweet-smelling sachet. She scowled and immediately threw the shiny sachet on the pavement and stamped on it for good measure. Ricardo could distinctly smell the coffee odour and stared down at the slimy, brownish pattern illuminated on the pavement and sighed deeply. Surely, he thought, this nasty congealed mess revealed pretty much everything to him.

The Midnight Mannequins

William was portly and always had a somewhat serious look about him. He lost most of his tufted hair in his forties and at seventy-nine, he felt a little sparse on top. His thick spectacles were usually smeared, and the light dusting of dandruff on his dark suit gave him a neglected and rather seedy look. His gait was still athletic, thanks to over thirty years of cross-country running. He carefully kept his 1970 county winner's trophy on the cluttered mantelpiece, even though the years had badly tarnished the cheap metal. The year 1970 was also very traumatic for William. By the end of that year, he had lost his job as a mathematics teacher, at Richmond School. The new Headmaster explained gently to William that, the boy's story had convinced the Governors that, he should go quietly. The '*story of my life,*' he thought, as he waved goodbye to Miss Henderson, the school secretary. He felt that she knew he was an innocent man, and that was far more important than the lump sum, which proved helpful, but rather insulting as the years had since revealed.

William arose early, splashed cold water on his face; he rarely, these days, looked in the bathroom mirror and after a vigorous towelling of his ruddy features, he crossed the hallway, into his small kitchen. Fresh coffee was a passion and he fussed over the making of every cup. As the percolator bubbled, it reminded him of Miss Celia Hopkins in her science laboratory at Richmond School. She had emigrated shortly after his untimely departure. He missed her laughter and eccentric habits. *It would be so nice*, he thought, *to bump into her again*. She had always made him laugh out loud: a rarity these days. He led an industrious yet isolated life, but he was a man who avoided regrets.

"Regrets kill people, Willy, and usually the good ones! So, avoid regrets, son." His mother, Enid, had been a great comfort to him, and her strong voice still reverberated around the kitchen with clarity. Enid and his father, Harry, had spent their lives in Richmond. Harry had occupied his last years as a Guide at Richmond Castle, and he was infamous for his tall ghost stories with the American tourists, in particular. In fact, he dropped dead in Richmond Castle, which Enid afterwards, joked, was the result of seeing the 'headless woman' he spent years preaching about. "The very chill down one's spine, even in the height of summer!" was repeated most evenings at teatime.

Their big house, overlooking the Castle and the meandering river Swale, was sold during the hot summer of 1971 at a very good price for North Yorkshire. William usually avoided passing it these days. It was a bed and breakfast establishment, which his mother would have loathed. He felt that strangers damaged those fond memories of his happy childhood. He was an only child but had never been spoilt. Enid made sure of that.

William's compact bungalow lay at the leafy end of a narrow cul-de-sac on the northern outskirts of Richmond town. He missed his childhood garden with its view of the castle ruins and the glistening river Swale. The river's calm moods and anger announced the seasons with a natural clarity. His neighbours these days were an odd bunch and there were nine staggered homes in all. He spoke to everyone he met, but they all pretty much minded their own business.

Routine suited William, but it also stifled him. Even at his age, he still needed to feel that something exciting or out of the ordinary would happen in his life. He poured coffee carefully into a red mug, followed by a little milk and went into his tiny, neat back garden. A small metal table with a solitary old chair sat under a lone sycamore tree. Summer mornings were precious to him, and he sat and slowly sank into the faded striped cushion. He sipped his coffee as if it were very expensive wine and listened to the birdsong. He could hear the couple next door arguing over silly things. Harold Smith had worked for the town council and his wife, Mavis, was a retired secretary; a word she hated and always used the title 'Personal Assistant' when the situation allowed. They had no children, as far as he knew and disliked all pets.

The Smiths argued every morning at breakfast time. They were masters of routine, which Mavis told William, was the recipe for a long and happy retirement. After all, they were both well into their seventies and they knew exactly what each day would bring: she had her jobs, and he had his 'to do list'.

"We are not ones for frivolous hobbies!" she remarked one day to William as they walked together to the town centre shops. Mavis allowed one very little time for interruption, so the secret was to simply listen. She enjoyed gardening and her husband had, what she called, his 'special talent'. Harold painted watercolours with very little creativity, but with tremendous vigour. Most of his art collection hung around every wall in their bungalow, and she forcefully reminded any admirers of his work that, he would never sell any of his creations. For whatever artistic reason, the backdrop to all his paintings featured the river Swale. "The Vicar once told me that I was living with a pure artistic genius, and I have never forgotten those words," she told William. He just nodded and smiled approvingly.

The previous Christmas, William had been presented with a small watercolour titled, 'River Swale in spring' and signed with an off-white, wide flourish by the artist. William disliked the work intensely and still remembers the cloud of depression hanging over him while all three of them ate Christmas lunch in their gloomy dining room. He counted twenty-three 'River Swales' proudly hanging on their pink rose-patterned wallpaper, Mavis remarked lightly while chewing on a piece of turkey breast, that she supposed it was a bit like having Christmas dinner in the National Gallery. William almost choked on his partially cremated turkey leg and just grinned ever so politely. Harold said that he had always wanted to visit London to see the galleries.

"Far too expensive," said Mavis quite bitterly.

"Most are free these days, by all accounts," said William cheerfully. "No running off to London, Harold, at our age. Too crowded for us country folk and we have all the art one could wish for right here. Retirement has made you restless dear," and Mavis took their plates at speed to the kitchen.

Both men chuckled and nodded before going into the cluttered living room to watch the Queen's speech.

Summer had a habit of disappearing like a close friend emigrating overseas. William sipped a glass of red wine in the garden, wrapped in an old pullover. He pondered on the good things in his life, and then his thoughts turned to the long, dark winter evenings, and the countdown on his kitchen calendar to Christmas. He knew it was almost time to bring his garden furniture indoors. The lavender plant in an old moss-covered pot swayed gently in the breeze. He closed his eyes to more fully appreciate the dying scent. "If only —" he sighed — "I had done more with my life." Celia Hopkins, he remembered, had once remarked: 'Normal people really worry me!' Her beautiful face would be lined by now, but he knew that, she would still make him laugh out loud; no one in the cul-de-sac ever made him smile these days.

In mid-November, Mavis told him excitedly, that the drapery store in Richmond was closing down. She suggested that he should go and stock up for the winter snows while pointing at the frayed sleeve of his pullover. He wasn't particularly interested, but on their last day of trading, he went in to take a final look at 'Price & Sons Outfitters' in the main square. It was a dank Saturday morning with a leaden feel, and no prospect of glimpsing a patch of blue sky. The neglected shop front window with peeling red paint and cobweb cartwheels hinted of good trading times long gone. His parents had known the Price family well, and their unmarried son, Bob, had decided to call it a day. The nearby 'Tesco Superstore', according to Mavis had pushed him to the brink. "Of course, being a bachelor at his age is also bad for business, especially in a Garrison town. People talk!" she had hastily remarked the previous Christmas while pouring lumpy gravy over their soggy Brussels sprouts.

The small store was very busy, but William was, nevertheless, greeted warmly by Bob, who always looked scruffy, and his shabby black suit contrasted with his shopkeeper's pale pallor. A thin, unwashed looking man; whose thick head of greying hair belied his years. William guessed that he was possibly only fifteen or twenty years his junior. Bob's younger sister, Sally, had drowned in the river Swale a few weeks before her wedding. Even though it was maybe thirty or more years ago, William could see great sadness in Bob's skeletal face. He brushed past a few of the customers sifting through piles of shirts and pullovers. It was only after Harold and Mavis left, with a large bag of shirts and underwear, that the idea struck William like a bolt of lightning.

"It's a sad day for us all, Bob. It can't be an easy one for you. I have such good memories of the early years when your dad stood always 'at attention' behind this very counter," and he touched the mahogany fondly. Bob shifted uneasily, and William detected a tear in his right eye. He blinked and said farewell to an elderly woman leaving empty handed.

"I will definitely miss this place. Old age, I suppose and to be honest, William, business of late has been poor. It's becoming a Bistro of some sort," and he sighed while tidying up loose ties on the counter.

"Bob, do you mind if we have a private word at the back of the shop?" Both men walked slowly towards a neat row of

19

seven or eight smartly dressed mannequins, to the left of the cramped changing cubicle.

"You may think that what I am about to say to you sounds a bit odd, Bob. But I wondered if you might consider selling me three of those mannequins. One male and two females are all that I would need." William began to stroke the nearest male mannequin looking somewhat embarrassed.

"Why, of course, William. You can have them for free God only knows what you can do with them?" and Bob guffawed, sounding a bit like their nervous new Vicar.

"I insist on paying you for them Bob and I will need them delivered. It has to be after dark. You never know what the neighbours would think, you see," and he smiled contentedly. The deal was done for a tenner and Bob promised to drop them off the following week.

As Christmas approached, William reduced his trips to the shops. He detested the season and its enforced jollity. Walking past 'Prices' shuttered store only added to the winter gloom. A notice taped to the main shop window stated, that the refurbishment work would commence in January 1994, in bold black letters. Once the new Bistro opened, he decided that he would take Harold and Mavis there to compensate them for his annual invitation to Christmas lunch. Harold called it dinner and was always scolded by Mavis, because when she was a Personal Assistant, she only ever marked dinners in her boss's diary. One always had to use correct terminology in her position.

They also included William in their New Year's Eve party, if you could call it that; its format never changed. Red wine in small glasses, a selection of canapés from the local

Co-op; a very dreary charades session to kill time until midnight, and then a lukewarm glass of Bucks Fizz. "It's only the three of us again, but we are alive and kicking!" Mavis gaily announced raising her glass every year and sipping the flat orange coloured liquid. Her rouge cheeks and glossy pink lipstick suggesting a lady of the night, now long retired.

William ate a simple lunch on New Year's Eve and was quite exhausted from the furtive happenings since his morning coffee. Mavis had called in breezily as expected, to ask if he had by any chance changed his mind. She apologised and remarked that, he must be terribly busy preparing for his guests. He received an unexpected peck on both cheeks before she left, and she winked or rather blinked in his direction while waving.

"Snow on the forecast, according to Harold. Hope your houseguests get here on time. Three of you; my, you will be a busy little bee! Anyway, you know where we are if they get stuck in the snow. I'm not quite ready for just the two of us at midnight. Bye dear."

William watched her slightly bent figure walk by his privet hedge until the plastic lantern by their front door burst into life and prompted him to quickly draw the blinds in his front room.

His parent's clothes lay stored in boxes in the cramped attic, and he cautiously scaled the loft ladder armed with an old torch. A random selection was made, including an old, feathered hat, which his mother wore for weddings and occasionally funerals; depending upon whom had died. Partridge feathers, and real ones at that, she used to proudly proclaim after the first sherry had been gulped down far too quickly. His father always retorted that they were blasted pheasant feathers, but was as usual, totally ignored.

A pungent smell of damp filled the room, and the electric fire caused a tiny cloud of steam to float above the odd pile of garments. William worked briskly and carried the three mannequins carefully from the ironing board storage cupboard. He dressed each mannequin with great care and even his father's favourite navy-blue tie was knotted with precision. He called the male mannequin 'John', and the two ladies became 'Annie' and 'Celia Hopkins'. Celia was given her full title and he placed the feathered hat with some reverence on her stiff curled wig of jet-black hair.

William then sat down with a mug of coffee and quietly inspected his creations. He chuckled at all three standing like 'wallflowers' at a noisy party by the four-bar electric fire. Through a small gap in the blind, he could see Harold and Mavis playing a game of whist. Normally at this hour, their heavy brown curtains would have been firmly drawn, but they appeared determined to watch for the arrival of William's guests.

"You are not listening to me, Harold." He put his hand of cards down and replied, "Of course, I'm listening to you dear. You just said that you didn't believe that William was having guests for New Year's Eve. Am I right?"

"Well, there was no smell of cooking earlier. There are no photographs in that home of his; just the one of his parents and his mother looking demented in that feathered hat. No wonder the man is so odd! However, I made it crystal clear that, he was always welcome here if they failed to make it through the snow."

"There is no snow, dear, and it's now gone seven."

Mavis gave him a scornful look and put her cards back carefully in the pack. "There will be snow before midnight. I'm off to 'do my face' and then prepare the canapés. It's a proper waste holding a party for just the two of us. My expensive bottle of 'Buck's Fizz' will be flat by morning, and you are not getting more than a glass. We both know what happened after you got a bit tipsy in 1986!"

The threatened snow clouds never arrived over Richmond and by 8 p.m., a starry sky sparkled above the darkened cul-de-sac. There was little sign of life, or anything unusual to indicate, that 1994 was mere hours away. The inhabitants gave scarce, if any, clues when it came to signs of merriment.

William hummed one of his favourite tunes in the kitchen and put a small dish of shepherd's pie in the microwave. He then poured out four glasses of sweet sherry, and very cautiously placed them on a stained silver tray. He carried them into the front room and put one of his J.S Bach compact discs on, at high volume. He sniggered while placing a glass near each of his guests. John and Annie stood, as if chatting amicably by the fireplace and he had reserved the sofa for Celia Hopkins whose sherry glass was that bit fuller than the others. He made some further adjustments to Celia's posture as she appeared to be in a somewhat arthritic pose. Then, he gulped down some sherry and circulated amongst his guests, taking sufficient time to chat to each in turn. This New Year's Eve party would certainly be one to remember.

The powerful peal of bells at midnight woke William from his slumber and he eased himself hurriedly away from the shiny face of Celia. Her feathered hat was at an unusual angle, and her wig had worked its way a little too high on her pale milky forehead. William stood rigidly by the blinds and raised an empty sherry glass in slow motion to all three guests.

A generous tear trickled down his left cheek as he, once again, remembered Celia Hopkins' infectious laughter.

How Is Your Mother?

Amelia Hamilton-Brown fussed repeatedly over the floral arrangement in the hallway with her usual energy and desire for perfection. A trim, rather severe countenance, hid a fun-loving creature who had devoted thirty or more years to her husband's military career. Donald, now a Group Captain, was in the final months of his last RAF posting as a Station Commander at a large, busy airbase in Lincolnshire. Only a few minutes earlier, she had kissed him goodbye and watched proudly as his car, with flying pennant on the bonnet, drove away from their imposing Officer's Married Quarter on Vulcan Drive.

Thoughts of retirement haunted her while she used her old gardening scissors to prune and freshen some withered blooms on her latest floral creation. The heady scent of Jasmine lifted her spirits, and she brushed all loose leaves and other debris into a wicker basket using an old goose wing; a trick she had inherited from her 'house proud' mother.

In the dining room, the sound of Mrs Crawford polishing the oak dining table comforted her greatly. This bat woman was a rare treasure, who ensured, that the house was pristine, yet homely. The Hamilton-Browns were renowned for their weekly dinner parties, and they entertained elegantly and always generously. She was a devoted service wife and had never given much thought to life beyond the 'guardroom gate', until now.

Their two sons went to Wadham College, Oxford and Max worked in the London stock exchange, whereas Richard, the creative one, was pursuing a career in the theatre. Donald did not approve of his youngest son earning little money as a stagehand in the West End. "One day, that boy will grow up and get a proper job!" he repeated almost weekly. Amelia was very protective of them both and bristled when he said such things. Being a Station Commander often drained him of compassion and she quickly forgave him.

There would be eight people around the oak table that evening, so she started a mental checklist of the final arrangements. Fridays were always such great days, and a good dinner party really christened their very well-deserved weekend break. Donald's workload was incredibly demanding, but she knew that when he finally stopped flying, the loss would affect them heavily. She was not quite sure how, but an uneasy air had invaded their lives. "Oh, it's nothing to worry about," she had confided in Richard during their last telephone call, but she knew he was not convinced.

He was her favourite son, and this of course she knew was wrong.

Mrs Crawford rarely needed prompting and by late morning, the table was laid, and she had placed a crisp white linen tablecloth over a garden table on the patio. Their old, patched canvas sun umbrella, that had survived postings to Malta, Germany and Cyprus, had been erected to provide shade for their two gleaming ice buckets. Eight glistening champagne glasses rested upside down in a square formation. The odd array of garden furniture had been adorned with various red and white striped cushions, which made the terrace somewhat reminiscent of Umbria.

The gnarled beech tree at the foot of their imposing garden filtered the August air and Amelia stood, admiring the scene under a gin clear sky.

Every day at eleven, the ladies took coffee together and Mrs Crawford wrote down any new tasks in the small black notebook she kept in the top pocket of her apron. She always addressed Amelia as 'ma'am' and the Group Captain as 'sir'. Any over familiarity made her feel uncomfortable; it was the way she had been brought up.

A little after 1 p.m., Mrs Crawford went to 'powder her nose,' a ritual which marked the end of her shift. Amelia stood in the dining room and waved her off. The old bicycle was rusty, but it supported its owner in all weathers. She refused to wear a helmet: "It plays havoc with my hair, ma'am. I rarely pedal very fast these days," was her usual retort. An accident with a new American hair dye, which she often stressed she used in the privacy of her home, had caused serious hair loss. Donald was convinced, that the woman wore a wig! Sometimes, after heavy rainfall, little droplets of black dye clung to her pale forehead and Amelia smiled knowingly. The lad from Estates and Buildings, who tended to their large garden, once remarked that poor Mrs Crawford should not be at work with a dose of measles.

Amelia started to put the place cards around the dining table, an important last ritual to ensure the evening was successful. Once she had very carefully positioned Wing

Commander Bunty Oakshot and his wife Felicity, she began to relax. Bunty was rather a sexist bore and Felicity was very partial to the gin bottle. Bunty was fiercely loyal to Donald and an incredibly bright and experienced Officer Commanding Operations, so Amelia easily tolerated his many foibles. She walked around the table a few times and then changed two of the place settings. It was best she thought to put the new Adjutant on XXV Squadron next to Felicity. This would be Flying Officer Nigel Barrington's first dinner party with the Station Commander, and she wanted him to feel at ease. Felicity's incessant laughter and tales of her tennis lessons always lightened the mood. Donald usually frowned and swore, that he would never play tennis again!

She 'tut-tutted' to discover a ninth place setting and was amused at having written 'Felicity Oakshot' out twice. She hid the spare white card etched in black in the drawer of their antique oak sideboard. *Strange*, she remarked, *the thought of leaving the RAF is making me muddled of late*. What with Donald's high blood pressure, recently diagnosed by the Station Medical Officer, this revelation meant he was not supposed to fly, and then her memory lapses; we are fast becoming 'two old fogies' they began to joke. There was a growing sadness behind the laughter, but neither of them would admit it.

Donald hid his daily tablets in the barrel of an old Browning pistol inherited from his father, who had been an Army Colonel. Every evening before dinner, he pointed the barrel towards his temple and pretended to shoot. The pistol was then lowered ceremoniously, and the pills were swiftly popped into his mouth. A mouthful of water and nothing more was said. This became the signal for Amelia to pour their wine.

Three years had elapsed since Donald left the RAF and Amelia's social diary had all but emptied, except for the most frivolous of engagements.

Civilian life was proving so much tougher than they had both envisaged. Mornings were the most challenging time of the day because of Donald's mood swings. It was on a frosty, clear morning in late October, that Amelia felt at her lowest ebb. Donald sat reading the job vacancies in the 'Daily Telegraph' with a forlorn look and stubble on his chin. In all of their years of marriage, she had never seen him unshaven.

"You will shave dear? Anyone may call at any moment." And she began to wash up the breakfast things. He removed his reading spectacles and gave her an irritated look.

"That's the second time Amelia that, you have asked me to shave this morning. Are you, by any chance, losing your marbles?"

She simply glanced out at the small garden and just smiled thinking back to those wonderful happy and busy days at Vulcan Drive. She didn't reply but went upstairs to make the beds in their separate bedrooms. His bedroom still contained all of his flying kit, hanging neatly in the wardrobe and his hat with 'scrambled egg' on the peak sat proudly on a desk by their wedding photograph. 'A match made in heaven,' her teary-eyed mother had blurted while watching them emerge from the gothic Church entrance under an archway of ten crossed swords, held ceremoniously by Donald's fellow aircrew in full uniform.

Suddenly, a black range rover drove at speed, right up to their front doorstep and Amelia watched excitedly while the driver removed her large sunglasses.

"Oh, Donald dear. Guess who has just arrived? It's Tabatha Burford-Brown."

"Oh, good God. I'm off to shower and shave dear. Can't stand that woman for more than five minutes. Tell her that, I'm up in London," and he sprinted upstairs.

Amelia quickly dried her hands and checked her hair in the hallway mirror. I'm looking jolly haggard she thought, as a tall, slim shadow appeared at the frosted glass panels of their front door.

"Darling, you look simply marvellous," and Tabatha gave her a crushing hug. An overpowering smell of Lavender wafted into the hallway and made Amelia gasp for breath.

"You are the one who looks divine, Clucky," said Amelia leading her into the living room. "We have not seen you since our farewell dinner party at Vulcan Drive. You and Andrew were ever so kind to give us that aerial photograph of our house on the airbase. There it is by the fireplace. Such wonderful memories."

"How is Donald? Andrew was hoping that he's now with British Airways and that you are once more home alone!" She crossed the room to the photograph and smiled.

"Donald is fine. We both still miss the RAF. Perhaps I miss it more that he does right now." Amelia noticed that Clucky had tilted the photograph carelessly and she corrected it before going into the kitchen to make coffee.

"So good to see you again, Clucky. Just like old times. Has Andrew left the service?"

"Good God, no darling. Whatever gave you that idea? He would be completely lost out of uniform." She sipped her coffee and listened to the taps running strongly upstairs.

"Oh, is Donald at home dear?"

"Oh yes, he's working from home today and should be down, shortly, if he ever finishes that report for the Ministry of Defence. He will be so pleased to see you and to hear your news."

"Andrew's been promoted and is now in Donald's big office. Darling Amelia, we live in your old house on Vulcan Drive. That Mrs Crawford is certainly a treasure. We want you both to come to our first dinner party on Friday. No excuses Amelia."

Donald heard the last part of their conversation as he padded to his bedroom clutching a towel. He was stunned to hear of Andrew's promotion. One of my worst pilots he muttered; just surprised that he is still alive! Life is often so unfair. Normally, he was a man who detested prying, but he left his bedroom door slightly ajar while changing into a smart business suit. He couldn't bear to think of Andrew in his Station Commander's office and living in their elegant old residence. "He will never run the airbase like I did," he whispered, "and as for that Tabatha woman, she will ruin his career in the end." He closely examined his freshly shaven chin and made another adjustment to his red polka dot tie. A handkerchief, of the same colour, was carefully placed in his top pocket. Then, he slowly paced the room listening to their energetic conversation with considerable discomfort.

"Donald is working on some urgent paper or other and hates any disturbance. Give him a few more minutes, Clucky. Why not stay to lunch?"

"Impossible darling. Our diary is not for the faint hearted," and she laughed, a little too loudly. "How are the boys doing? They must be grown men by now," and she took her coffee cup into the kitchen. Amelia followed her and put the sugar bowl in the fridge, which struck Tabatha as a rather peculiar thing to do. She was on the verge of mentioning it but thought better of such a sensitive intrusion.

"Before I forget Tabatha, how is your mother?"

Tabatha sat slowly into the wooden rocking chair by the comforting Aga cooker.

"Amelia dear, surely you must remember that my mother's been dead for a good three years or more. You and Donald were our saviours back then. Vulcan Drive became my 'second home'."

"I'm dreadfully sorry Clucky, please forgive me. Promise that you will not mention a word of this to anyone? I've not been myself of late. I don't think Donald has noticed. Richard keeps joking that his dear mother has gone demented!" And she laughed rather nervously while escorting Tabatha to her car. She stood waving on the doorstep and said, "I promise that we will be there on Friday evening, Clucky. It will be such a treat to see our old house once more." She then went to get the garden rake to rid the gravel of Tabatha's heavy tyre marks before Donald created a scene. Donald was no longer the man she had married, and she stopped by the garage door staring vacantly at the healthy herbaceous borders, always her pride and joy.

Jolly Good Show

Nigel was a happy, rather eccentric, middle-aged man, or so it seemed to the many customers who frequented his small Bistro in Durham city. He had been to boarding school, served in the Army, worked in a London Bank, sailed private yachts in the Caribbean, and was now the proud owner of Bistro 13 at fifty-five and a bit years old. He actually rented the premises, due to a recent divorce settlement. He told those who asked, with a ready smile, that his wife, Fenella, had run off with a penniless, but very handsome Italian waiter.

Customers loved his tales more than his cooking, but he made delicious, scrambled eggs on granary toast with a large chunk of smoked salmon; his 'house speciality' and a firm favourite of the student fraternity. This was usually washed down with strong fresh coffee every morning and at lunchtime, and well into the evening with a good glass of Chablis. His prices were modest, the surroundings very elegant and opera was played incessantly throughout the day. Rumours quickly spread that Nigel had no interest or need to make a profit; this was simply a hobby. A big blackboard above the corner bar pronounced in beautiful white chalk handwriting: "What is life without fresh eggs, good wine and opera!" It acted as a constant focus for his loyal clientele and appeared to always lighten the mood, even in the dreariest weather in the North of England.

One of the attractions and at times frustrations was that Nigel never stuck to formal opening times and he was always closed when he sailed his modest yacht from Holy Island on Mondays and Tuesdays. Usually, by 10 a.m., on a Wednesday morning, he carefully opened the robust wooden shutters and laughed loudly as customers came through the bright green door. One was welcomed by the smell of reputable ground coffee, fresh flowers on the counter and the melodic strains of the first opera recital of the day: usually Mozart at that hour.

Nigel was very respectable looking, with neatly trimmed grey hair, flashing blue eyes and a distinguished pencil moustache. It was sometimes said that he clipped his eyebrows too often for a man. He would never allow customers to select from his enviable opera collection, all neatly stacked between the big aluminium coffee machine and the gin and wine bottles. A tall Cathedral style candle dripped wax on to the counter throughout each day. The candle flame was as important a ritual to Nigel as his beloved opera music.

Dr Olive Pomeroy lived nearby and took great pride in always being one of his first customers. She wore a black shiny raincoat in all weathers and a faded pink beret. She peered rather severely at Nigel over her tiny round spectacles when ordering her eggs and salmon. She had a coffee allergy, which prompted her to have the first alcoholic drink of the day well before noon. Olive was a retired librarian now well into her seventies and with a voracious appetite for opera. She often repeated to Nigel her love for the word 'spinster' and like her twin sister, sadly now long dead; she had never particularly taken to men.

The Bistro had seven tables and Olive usually claimed ownership of table number three overlooking the cobbled street. Her stained raincoat, once neatly folded, was placed carefully on the spare wooden chair, as if it were a cushion. Only when the Bistro was full at lunchtime, did Olive ever agree to share her very private space. Her icy stare and prolonged silence usually worked wonders and the students or locals who dared join her, normally fled after choking on hastily eaten food. "No manners these days!" was her frequent retort to those vacating the chair. It was quite normal practice for Olive to sit through three or four opera recitals before slowly making her way home to feed her cat 'Thimble'.

Nigel had known Olive for over three years, but she rarely revealed anything of importance. Her father had been a dentist in Ireland before the family emigrated to London, and ultimately to Durham. Thimble was now her constant and only companion, and Olive had travelled regularly to Central America as a young Anthropologist. Her knowledge of the tribes in that region was legendary, but she normally offered very measured responses when asked. The one customer Nigel knew who irked Olive greatly was Brigadier French. He was a very loud and rather pompous man with a most impressive knowledge of opera. Nigel loved to eavesdrop when they argued over a particular piece of music, and he sometimes forgot what customers had ordered when Wagner encouraged heated debate from table three.

It was a sunny, cheerful Friday morning and the Brigadier marched into the busy Bistro with his usual panache.

"Good morning, everyone." He snorted and smiled broadly in Nigel's direction. "A terrific opera, old boy. I could listen to Bellini all day long, but no time, sadly, for such frivolous pursuits. Listening properly to opera is a very serious business indeed."

He was clad in his usual tweed jacket with black leather patches on the elbows and he wore an immaculately creased pair of cavalry twill trousers. 'Once cut a finger on my trouser creases, old boy,' he often remarked to nobody in particular. His red and navy striped tie was knotted with precision, and a yellow handkerchief protruded teasingly from his left breast pocket. Olive likened it to a crushed pansy and sighed deeply before removing her coat from the spare chair.

"Good afternoon, Brigadier. I presume you will need this reserved seat?" and she grinned, showing no real sign of the deep irritation his sudden arrival had caused.

"Jolly good show. How lovely to see you, Olive dear. Thanks so much." She hated being called 'dear', but the Brigadier was not a man to correct. He settled into the chair and asked Nigel even more loudly for his usual. He studied Olive's empty wine glass for a few moments and surveyed the animated students at the surrounding tables.

"Are you about to depart, Olive?" and he adjusted the chair to enable Nigel to pour him a generous glass of Chablis.

"Do you mean am I about to die, Brigadier?" she remarked somewhat caustically.

"I say, old girl, steady on. I simply assumed that your empty wine glass and plate meant you had finished. Your lunch has perhaps ended, that's all I actually meant. Do have a Chablis on me, Olive," and he had ordered it rather too loudly, before she could even reply.

"Cheers Brigadier," said Olive and she sipped her wine sparingly. She would tolerate the pompous oaf for a further hour or so, she thought. She pitied his poor wife, even though she had never met her. One of the boys at the next table turned and raised his coffee cup. "Cheers Brigadier. Great opera, don't you think?"

The Brigadier glared at him and his giggling friend. "All opera is great, I will have you know, young man." And he spread the linen serviette carefully over his lap.

"How is your dear wife today, Brigadier?"

"How very kind of you to ask, Olive. Not too well, I'm afraid. Camilla suffers from frightful mood swings and has done so ever since we returned from Burma. That must be well over thirty years ago now. She was attacked by a mad dog and has never been herself since. All most unfortunate; took to the gin bottle for quite some time. Oh dear, do forgive me, Olive. Far too much dreary, domestic detail at this hour of the day," and he took a swig of Chablis and tucked into his plate of salmon and scrambled eggs.

Olive appreciated the spectacle of the Brigadier enjoying his food and making random murmuring noises in the process. Her mealtimes were rather a sad ritual, except of course for Thimble, who watched every morsel being eaten from his lumpy armchair cushion. Olive's appetite was usually much improved by the happy chatter and opera at Bistro 13.

"I find, I eat much more when I'm out than at home, Brigadier," uttered Olive, and she then regretted this tiny revelation.

"Oh, I say, old girl, I must agree with you. However, I take most of my meals with Camilla. I wouldn't actually call them jolly affairs but needs must!" and he laughed and adjusted his tie, before draining his wine glass.

"Of course, you will have become very used to eating alone, Olive, I dare say?"

"Yes, quite Brigadier. Thimble keeps me company, of course," and she looked annoyed at the invasive noise from a nearby table.

"Would you perhaps care to join us for a fondue supper next Monday?" and he eagerly removed a small diary from his inner jacket pocket.

Olive was already aware of these fondue rituals, which she had deftly managed to miss for well over a year. Nigel warned her that the evening was a very dreary affair, and best avoided at all costs. Camilla was usually pretty drunk, and she kept dropping melted blobs of some obscure cheese on his jacket sleeve. "Dreadful, never again," he had whispered one morning at the counter.

"Thanks so much, Brigadier. Monday is my bridge evening. Such a shame, but possibly another time," said Olive feeling very ashamed of lying. "Yes, of course. Certainly," and he tucked his diary away. "I had absolutely no idea that you played bridge, Olive. Do forgive my impertinence, but you don't look like a bridge player to me."

Olive glanced around the Bistro, quite unsure as to how she might respond, but she then decided that silence was best.

Nigel watched them from behind his cramped bar and thought the Brigadier and Olive appeared to have become the perfect couple. They were now laughing easily together, and Olive had removed her mustard-coloured cardigan. Her slender, lily-white arms rested on the tabletop, and he saw her at least once or twice attempt to conduct the opening score to 'The Magic Flute'. The four glasses of wine she had already drunk helped to erase any previous tension with the Brigadier. He had never heard Olive chuckling so freely, and it pleased him to see some colour and vitality return to her usually drawn features. Her ill-fitting dentures caught the rays of sunshine when she laughed; this was not a good advertisement he thought for her family's dental pedigree.

She would have been a stunner in her youth, Nigel imagined, as he made more coffees for table six. He was genuinely interested in his regulars, and he didn't like to think of Olive going back home each day alone. Bistro 13 and Thimble were vital parts of her daily life and perhaps, helped Olive to grow old with greater purpose and dignity.

October brought torrential rain and the River Wear burst its banks in places. Olive had been indoors for almost a week with Thimble and when the rainfall finally stopped on a Friday morning, she decided to escape to Bistro 13 for lunch. The Cathedral bells struck noon in the clear air as she locked her front door and popped the rusty key in her handbag. Olive had just started to use her umbrella as a walking stick on the smooth, slippery cobble stones, when she saw her nosey neighbour, Mrs Gillian Blake, approaching at a most unusual speed for her bulky frame. She looked flustered, so Olive greeted her warmly.

"I'm sorry, Miss Pomeroy to give you bad news. It's your cat, you see. The name is clearly on the collar with your telephone number. I didn't want to ring you," and Mrs Blake put the plastic carrier bag down on the cobbles.

"It was gone ten when I let him out of the house. Is Thimble dead, Mrs Blake?" uttered a very distressed Olive.

"I'm afraid so, dear. He's just been run over by a delivery van. A young man picked him up and we put his little body in this carrier bag. Please don't look inside dear, he's in quite a state from the tyres."

Olive simply nodded and thanked Mrs Blake for her kindness before carefully picking up the carrier bag. She noticed that the label said, 'Marks & Spencer' and it felt so light to carry. Thimble had been such a well-fed cat; so, when she had walked a little distance, she peered inside. The shock of seeing his bloodied and crushed little face affected her deeply. Instead of taking him home, she turned in a trance and made her way to Bistro 13.

Through her tears, she watched Nigel, bustling at his coffee machine, and for the first time in her life, she was actually pleased to see the Brigadier already sipping wine and humming away to the opera music. She knew that she could trust the Brigadier with his vast army experience, to deal with Thimble's remains, and she ever so quietly prayed that he might still invite her to one of his infamous fondue parties.

"Jolly good show!" said the Brigadier when Olive entered, and he sprang up briskly to pull out the spare chair for her.

The Price Tag

Herbert stood at the wooden gate to their thatched cottage front garden and sniffed the early morning air like a bloodhound. Dappled sunshine formed an umbrella shape under the thick set wisteria which his wife, Maude, had prodigiously cultivated since they first moved into 'Diamond Cottage' in the summer of 1976. He remembered that it had been an unusually hot summer, and his daily commute to London visibly drained him of energy. He came home irritable and smelly, but once he had taken a bath and accepted a cold gin and tonic from Maude, his large cottage in Oxley was a haven from his stressful desk at Barclays Bank on the Strand.

Herbert was by now a seasoned investment banker with no desire to either waste money or to live lavishly like some of his colleagues. They did not drive or own a car but had purchased two old Raleigh bikes in a nearby market during the long, hot summer of 1976. Herbert was a thickset man, not very tall, but it was said that he had his mother's flawless skin. This, he regarded as an old-fashioned sort of compliment. He wore suits from Jermyn Street, but he was equally happy to rummage in the London charity shops for bargains. He was blessed with good eyesight for all of his sixty-five years, despite a lifetime of poring over figures, graphs and financial tables.

This particular Friday morning, in late July, was a very special one. He removed the bicycle clips from his battered briefcase and very carefully folded each trouser leg. Maude stood at the cottage half door and her white pearl necklace glittered in the warm sunshine. She had a somewhat regal air about her and looked much older than her seventy years. Life had been good to Maude, except that she had always wanted children. The problem was Herbert, but such a delicate matter was never once discussed. It was totally off limits.

Before mounting his bicycle, Herbert jauntily plucked one of the crimson climbing roses and stuck it in his jacket lapel. He tilted his head slightly to the left and nodded towards the delicate rose head with approval. Maude waved him off in silence and remained at the door until he disappeared from view, at the foot of the hill. She examined her precious rose bush and picked up the stray petals from the mossy pathway. He had never worn a rose to work before, but she was so proud of her husband and knowing that this was his last day at the bank, she tried to imagine how he must feel. *He will return after 7 p.m.*, she thought with an engraved carriage clock destined already for the guest room. They had no desire to be drearily reminded every day of his retirement.

They were very comfortably off and Maude had already made a list of plans to fill Herbert's retirement. There would be seashore picnics and trips to hear opera at Glyndebourne, interspersed with weekends in Venice and romantic villages along the rugged Amalfi coast. They would both redesign the cottage garden and Herbert had always wanted a fishpond with carp. A business trip to Tokyo with the bank had influenced and nurtured his interest in carp, and a desire to add elements of a Zen Garden at the rear. Maude had never quite grasped his Eastern intentions. Whatever Herbert wanted, no matter how eccentric, Maude was always eager to help him realise his dreams. She had no interest in his financial career but was now keen to embrace the unhurried lifestyle that beckoned.

Herbert began to pedal slowly when he reached the small sign for the railway station indicating a further three miles. He usually caught the seven thirty to Paddington, but was happy to watch its sleek, twisting shape thundering through the early morning mist. He mopped his forehead with a crisp handkerchief before dismounting. He had just opened the little gate which led to a leafy path, that after about one hundred yards dropped suddenly and steeply down to the main railway lines, when a lady appeared briskly walking a black Labrador. Herbert, being a very polite man, bade her 'Good Morning'. This was ignored and it saddened him. He felt depressed in the sunshine, as he watched her frumpy figure disappear into a patch of woodland. On this, of all mornings, it mattered greatly to him, to have heard even a simple, friendly greeting.

He locked the rear wheel with his customary care and attention and left the bicycle leaning against one of the sturdy oak trees. He then placed his bicycle clips in the front pocket of his briefcase. He knew as he set off towards the railway line that it would take him just over ten minutes to reach the tracks. He stopped to mop his brow again and stuck his nose into an unknown wild shrub. The intensely sweet almost honey-like smell was a new one, but he found it very satisfying and quite intoxicating. Maude would have known exactly what it was he thought, and he stood savouring the moment. Even the birdsong pleased him, and he began to regret all of his rushed, early morning journeys over the years. This was the very first time he had ever changed the routine of his morning commute. The pathway began to narrow, and he did his best to avoid damaging his city suit on the whitethorn bushes brushing aggressively into his briefcase. By the time he had reached the clearing near the busy railway lines, he was completely out of breath. Only Herbert knew that his cancer had weakened him considerably, but for Maude's sake, he had stuck rigidly to cycling in all weathers.

His kindly, but slightly eccentric Professor at the Royal Marsden Hospital advised him to tell Maude at the very latest, after he retired. "Your wife must be told," the Professor had uttered when showing Herbert out of his clinic after the last consultation. He remembered replying, "Of course, Professor Girdler. I promise to break the news to Maude over a gin and tonic one evening, very soon," and then looking away rather sheepishly.

Herbert finally got to the clearing, and he was relieved that there was nobody in sight. He now heard the muffled rumble of traffic from the motorway, and strangely the birdsong from his new location was much clearer than earlier. He dabbed his forehead very gently and carefully removed his tie. After placing the tie and his wallet in the briefcase, he knelt down on the sun-scorched grass and said a short prayer. He looked studiously at his watch face and knew that he had just over three minutes remaining. He felt particularly calm, but his heartbeat had increased, and his mouth was dry; *a drink of cold water would have been nice*, he thought as he clambered carefully over the robust fence, tearing a precious suit sleeve in the process. He made the sign of the cross before lying down on the railway track. The increased vibration made him make a very slight adjustment to his head and neck. Herbert then simply closed his eyes for the last time and waited.

Maude's younger sister, Dorothy, invited herself for Christmas that year. Over five months had passed since Herbert's death, but Maude ideally wanted to face that first Christmas alone. It was not to be, and Dorothy arrived in her British, racing green-coloured MGB Roadster from Brighton on a cold, wet Sunday afternoon. Maude peeked from behind the heavy red curtains of the living room and observed how badly her sister had parked.

She checked that the soup pot was simmering nicely before unbolting the creaking front door latch.

"Oh, dear Maude. You have lost far too much weight. I will fatten you up sister dear over the next two weeks." And Dorothy threw her car keys carelessly on the surface of the long hallway chest of drawers. Two whole weeks gulped Maude, as she gingerly kissed the rouge-covered cheeks of her sister. Dorothy then, darted back into the heavy rain and pulled a large trunk-like device from the partially closed boot. Herbert had never quite warmed to Dorothy. He strongly disapproved of her short skirts and plucked eyebrows. "A trollop is what she is," he once said, after too much champagne, one Christmas Day.

Diamond Cottage was proving to be a wonderful sanctuary for Maude. She retained clear and incredibly resonant memories of Herbert. It often felt as if he was alive, and she was still in the habit of preparing two strong gins every evening; she drank them both, of course. Now Dorothy had invaded her precious space. She sighed while pouring their soup into bone china bowls with a deep purple edge. The steam fogged up her tiny spectacles and Dorothy was already making quite a din upstairs while unpacking.

"Dorothy dear, your soup is on the table," she shouted up the narrow stairs. She had almost said 'Herbert dear!' before checking herself, and a tear began to glisten in her right eye. Dorothy had donned a long and ill-fitting heavy cardigan. Bright lemon with black dice certainly didn't suit her age or complexion. *She has put on a lot of weight and looks positively sickly,* thought Maude, as her sister claimed the chair at the head of the kitchen table.

"No wine, dear?" enquired Dorothy and she started to make quite nauseous slurping sounds. She ignored the linen serviette that Maude had placed so carefully by her butter knife and plate. 'No breeding' was Herbert's usual retort when guests failed to use their serviettes. She could hear his polished tone and she studied Dorothy's ravenous antics while sipping the comforting homemade oxtail soup. It would last until Christmas Eve she imagined. Soup always tasted better when reheated.

By the end of lunch, Dorothy had brought her up-to-date on her exciting, single life in Brighton. The word boyfriend had caused her to stop eating, as it was not a word suited to Dorothy's age group. A man friend would have sounded so much better; she was after all in her late sixties. Herbert had increasingly disliked her, as in his words: she was 'far too flighty'. "Percival lives in the flat next-door, Maude. It's a relationship of convenience for me, dear. He spends oodles of money on his darling, Dotty. That's what he calls me, dear," and she pushed her empty soup bowl away. "No sex involved, which suits me fine as the much younger partner. He must be eighty, if not more, dear."

Maude ignored the sex remark and made an excuse to wash up. Dorothy remained seated, but her eye quickly caught sight of the heavy carriage clock above the fireplace. She removed her spectacles to read the shiny engraving to Herbert from the Bank on a small brass plate. She took a closer look at the back of the clock and was rather surprised to see a price tag still attached. It peeled off rather too easily and she returned to her chair to examine it more closely. "Good God, after all those years of hard work," she muttered before screwing it up into a tiny ball.

"Do you like the clock, Dorothy?" enquired Maude as she sat down wearily in Herbert's favourite armchair. Dorothy had already claimed her usual spot. "It's now a constant reminder to me of Herbert, rather than a mere retirement gift, if that makes any sense?" She folded her thin arms. "It will have cost the Bank a tidy sum, I feel sure. Herbert was held in very high esteem by all accounts. One of the seniors, a tidy, chubby sort of man, personally drove up from London to present it to me."

Dorothy nodded in agreement and flicked the price tag pellet into the grate. The flames devoured it, as if it was an unwelcome tumour. She kicked off her pink slippers and the dancing flames were soon reflected in her glossy red toenails. The stale, cheesy odour that emanated caused

Maude to flinch and return to the kitchen, to prepare a pot of tea. She looked into the well-groomed rear garden as darkness descended and the thatched gazebo began to lose its shape in the unfolding winter gloom. Maude pondered on the many summer Sundays she had sat under its shade with the newspapers, while Herbert prepared gins before Sunday lunch. He never shaved on Sundays, and she admired that almost daring side to the man she loved. A hint of stubble usually aroused her, but she ignored such fanciful notions, especially at her age. Retirement was, after all, what they had both planned with absolute precision. Now, she was a lonely widow, and those plans were in ruins.

She scalded the teapot and heard Dorothy say something from the front room. "I couldn't quite hear you, Dorothy," and she wedged the door open. A hidden voice from the tall fireside armchair said: "Do you remember what I said to you and Herbert only a few Christmases ago? I said clearly back then that it is impossible to put a price tag on retirement. Little did we know dear the impact of those words!" Maude busied herself by pouring their tea and she had decided to cut the Christmas cake early. It was just a tiny gesture of defiance, but she knew that it would lead to a very different year ahead. She handed Dorothy her tea and her broad smile was perfectly illuminated by the fire.

"I must say I'm quite shocked by how happy you look Maude. Are you unwell, dear?" asked a rather distracted looking Dorothy.

"Never felt better in my life, sister dear." And she threw her china cup and saucer into the fireplace. The spitting of the flames caused a tiny cloud of ash to fall on Dorothy's outstretched feet.

"My New Year's resolution will be to spend, spend and spend! Will you join me?" and she laughed hysterically with wild eyes, that received a frightening sort of glaze from the firelight.

"Not sure I would wish to see you waste Herbert's life savings, dear. Let me fetch you a sedative. We can talk more over Christmas; just the two of us. Like old times again, dear." With that she was gone, and Maude closed her eyes and relished the warmth of the flames and thought only of the good times ahead.

Love Letter

Miss Betty Murphy lived in total squalor but loved opera. Ever since she had taken her first unsteady steps into the local Church of 'St Mary the Virgin' in the village of Dooneen at about the age of three and heard the choir, something quite magical ignited within her. Tom and Maureen Murphy were staunch Catholics and strict parents to Betty and her older brother Sheamus. When Betty tried to sing along with the Church choir, on that spring morning back in 1955, she was told to behave; even her brother, at six years old, gave her a sharp slap.

The Murphy family lived with her father's mother in an old farmhouse by the river Blackwater. It was generally poor-quality land and the fields surrounding the house often flooded. Betty prayed for heavy rain, because it meant a boat ride downstream to the village shop which also acted as a pub and post office. It was Sheamus, who usually rowed home after their father had a few pints of Guinness with neighbours. Once little Betty was allowed to row, but her father grunted that they were too close to the tree-lined bank of the swollen river. Betty soon got used to the title of 'good for nothing' and often wiped away her tears when no one was looking.

In her teens, Betty thought little of her looks, but the smartly dressed photographer from Dublin, who took the annual school photographs, commented to the Mother Superior on Betty's striking good looks. For years, those three words reminded Betty, that she might stand a chance of singing on stage, or even acting in movies. The O'Leary's, who lived on the next farm, had a distant cousin who was a child actress in Hollywood.

She combed and brushed her long red hair every evening and thought of being on stage at the Royal Opera House in London. Her most cherished possession had been an old and faded programme of 'La Traviata,' which Mrs O'Leary had given her for her thirteenth birthday.

Then, one Sunday after Mass, Sheamus entered her tiny bedroom and threw the programme into the river. She still remembered the look of glee on his freckled, chubby face, as she approached the small bridge. He waved the now yellowing programme about, and then tossed it flapping into the fast-flowing river.

"Opera is shit and your singing is shit!" he shouted before striding off to milk their small herd of twenty cows. Betty had stood alone on the ivy-covered bridge and cried while the wind and the torrential rain stung her red cheeks. She remembered her long hair feeling heavy, as she passed the milking parlour. Her parents and Sheamus sat on wooden stools with their heaving backs turned to her.

"Of course, Betty's talent and ambitions for the stage should not be seen as odd, Mrs Murphy. There is nothing wrong with your daughter." The words of the kindly village GP, Dr Padraic Loneregan, who had a secret passion, it was rumoured for whisky and opera most evenings of the week.

Whenever Dr Loneregan met Betty in Church, he always encouraged her to sing, and one Sunday after the late Mass, he gave her a collection of old records in a faded blue covered box with a little brass lock and key. One of the records he told her was of Verdi's 'La Traviata': his favourite opera. She managed to smuggle the box into her bedroom without Sheamus knowing, and she planned to ask her father if he would buy her a second-hand record player. She knew that money was always short. Sheamus had post office savings, but she was far too scared to even mention her greatest wish to him.

When her grandmother died, the family inherited about ten thousand pounds and her mother insisted that Betty would get a new record player, which cost ten pounds and five shillings at Dunne's Stores in Cork. The years passed by quickly, but Betty never once got tired of listening to her coveted record collection. On summer evenings, with the half door open, sweet sounds from some of the world's best opera houses drifted down the fields to the riverbank and many of the garden birds appeared to Betty to sing along precisely in tune.

Her parents died within weeks of each other during a very harsh winter in 1994. Betty was about forty years old, considered locally, a spinster for life, and had no choice but to continue living at the farmhouse with her brother. Sheamus was a very moody and unhappy man and he treated Betty with utter disdain. She was now the maid, and he never displayed any form of affection towards her. He had become a rugged, scruffy and overweight individual with very few local friends. He drank heavily each Sunday and she dreaded hearing his heavy boots coming up the farm track. Their loyal sheepdog, 'Rover', always announced his master's unsteady arrival, and Betty would rush around preparing his roast meat and boiled potatoes for their Sunday evening meal.

Betty was banned from cycling into the weekly dances held in Dooneen village hall, and opera had not been allowed in the house since 1994. The old house, the prolonged bouts of wet, dreary weather and lack of happiness soon took their toll on Betty. She even stopped going to Sunday Mass.

Then, during a lovely hot summer's Sunday in 1997, she was introduced by Dr Loneregan to a new Guard posted to the village, after one of her rare appearances at Mass. Guard Kevin Daly was maybe ten years her junior, if not more, but once he had shaken her hand and smiled intensely at her, she felt quite faint. He had piercing blue eyes and suntanned skin, which were further enhanced by his wearing of a smart Guard's navy uniform.

"I must say Betty, that you and Kevin have, coincidentally, a love of opera in common, so I will leave you to chat. I must be off now to make a house call." They were hastily abandoned on the steps to the Church, and Kevin's generous smile and handsome face kept staring into hers. She could feel her cheeks flush, but it was a wonderful, new sensation and one, that she desperately wanted to last. Suddenly, Sheamus appeared and grunted that they must be getting off home. He looked Kevin up and down in a strange manner, almost as if he was studying a prize bull at a country show.

"No, no. He's my older brother," she managed to say, breathlessly, before Kevin rode off on his sturdy black bicycle. He kept glancing back, and she waved foolishly with the sun in her eyes.

"Get in the car, woman!" Sheamus shouted at her.

"Guard Daly lodges in the village with Mrs Broderick. No fancy ideas, Betty. He's far too young for the likes of you. For Christ's sake, I need an old spinster like you to look after me." They drove on in silence and her lips trembled. It felt as if she had left an opera performance against her will, without ever seeing or hearing the vitally important last act.

By the end of summer, she became more withdrawn and careless with her appearance and the housework. She sometimes dipped her breakfast things in a sink of cold, greasy water and used them for their midday meal. Her hopes of seeing Guard Kevin Daly faded, but she prayed every evening that one day he might ride his bicycle out to the farm.

On a frosty, clear morning, about a week before Christmas, the postman dropped off a few Christmas cards. A beautiful card with snow on mountains by a shimmering lake was from Guard Daly. The message in elegant handwriting said: 'Happy Christmas Betty. Please God we will meet early in the New Year. Why don't we try to listen to an opera together? Kevin.' Her hands shook and she took the card and envelope to her bedroom in the musty attic.

Sheamus was very irritated by the sudden change in her and was confused by her smile and neat appearance again. By Christmas Day, the farmhouse was scrubbed spotlessly clean and the polished windowpanes sparkled in the weak winter sunshine.

Christmas Day passed peacefully, but it was the first time that Betty missed Mass on Christmas morning. A heavy snowfall late on Christmas Eve made the farm track almost un-passable for vehicles. Sheamus took out the pony and trap and she avoided the freezing journey by making some feeble excuse. The O'Leary's had called in briefly for a Christmas drink by the fire and casually mentioned that Guard Daly was being moved to Limerick.

"What's wrong with you, woman?" growled Sheamus while chewing a goose leg across the table. *He's not even got any manners*, thought Betty and at that moment, she knew, that she truly hated her brother. She remained composed and even tried to smile while remembering happier Christmases from her childhood. Her heart was broken by the news of Guard Daly, and as she did the washing up, she devised a love letter in her head. Sheamus had already milked the herd of cows and was snoring by the large log fire. When she crept back in to join his bulky shadow, the sour smell from his discarded wellingtons made her feel sick. She sat in silence by the flames and mentally corrected the love letter. Rover opened an eye, licked her outstretched hand and wagged his long tail.

By New Year's Day, she had written out the relatively short love letter and was a bit embarrassed by how bold some of her words had been. The envelope was sealed tenderly in her bedroom, and she addressed it to his lodgings in Dooneen. She knew that Mrs Broderick could be trusted to hand it personally to him.

Sheamus was in a good mood and had even bothered to shave for the New Year's Eve drinks in the village pub. Betty was happy to stay at home with Rover and trusted Sheamus to drop her letter off at Mrs Broderick's house. He tucked it very carefully into the inner pocket of his heavy overcoat and smiled as he wished her a Happy New Year. Betty went upstairs and placed 'La Traviata' on the record player, and within minutes, she was waltzing around an empty Opera House stage held closely by the strong arms of Guard Daly. A little before midnight, she combed her red hair and noticed the increasing streaks of grey with a surge of sadness.

April was a particularly warm and sunny month, but still no news came from Guard Daly. The shadows of winter had left the thatched farmhouse and surrounding fields, and Betty fed the chickens pondering about Sheamus going to London that coming weekend. The cows had been sold and there was a very empty feeling about the place. This would be the first time in her life that she actually lived alone. Freedom from her brute of a brother became less appealing as the Saturday morning approached. Sheamus planned to stay with their Uncle Ned in London while looking for manual work.

Betty woke very early on the Saturday morning, but decided to spend a few extra minutes in her warm bed. She wanted to give Sheamus a good Irish breakfast before his long train and boat journey to a country she had only read about. It was seeing his suitcase in the kitchen the night before that reminded her that he was the first member of the farmhouse to travel abroad. Rover had been sitting and fretting all evening by the suitcase, sensing that something was up.

Suddenly, a single shot rang out from the barn causing her heart to leap and she jumped out of bed. She lifted the net curtain on her upstairs bedroom and saw Sheamus carrying a plastic animal feed sack across the yard. It was when he turned in the early morning light, towards the bridge that she saw the limp tail of Rover, trailing in the muddy farmyard. She sat back on the hard bed and waited for the dizzy spell to pass. Betty remained silent in her room, until Sheamus picked up his suitcase and shouted: "God bless, Betty. Keep the old home safe and sound for my return, one day." The door banged shut and it was then that her madness began in earnest.

Late that afternoon, still in her nightclothes, she ventured outside and walked slowly to the bridge. Her hair billowed in the breeze, as she looked down at the fast-flowing current. The water was crystal clear, and the sack had become tangled in the drooping branch of a tree. Her sense of hopelessness and numbness increased when her eyes also caught sight of her coveted collection of records glinting like fish scales on the slippery stone surface. They had all been smashed to smithereens.

Possibly, ten or more years had passed, and Betty was rarely seen beyond the farmhouse. She lived off her vegetable patch and chickens, and the kind O'Leary's continued to bring her groceries from the village, and further afield. The random, cold postcards from London had stopped, but she was glad and often prayed that Sheamus would never come home.

On a glorious summer's day in 2007, Betty received a surprise visitor. She heard a car approaching and quickly removed her filthy, food-stained apron. Her half door was open, and she stepped nervously into the sunshine trying to tuck her wild, grey hair into the collar of her tattered cardigan. It was a very feeble looking Dr Loneregan who greeted her, and she welcomed him into her kitchen. He tried not to show his shock at the filthy state of Betty and her domestic surroundings. The putrid smells were the worst he had ever encountered during his long lifetime as a GP.

When she cleared away a pile of debris to enable him to sit, he smiled to see the old record player. Almost as if reading the old man's mind, Betty said: "Only one record has survived, Dr Loneregan. La Traviata, my favourite!" and she went to make him some tea.

"What brings you to the wilds, Dr Loneregan?" she asked somewhat earnestly.

"Don't bother with tea, Betty. Thanks all the same. I heard in the village that you are often being disturbed and pestered by the older boys. It has worried me, and I told Father Casey that I wanted to see you anyway." Betty sat down and wiped her dirty hands on the cardigan. Tears glistened in those powerful blue eyes, and she simply shrugged her shoulders. Neither of them could speak for about ten minutes. The only brief interruption came from hen's pecking at grain by the open door.

"Just insults and they throw the odd stone at my windows. They usually shout: 'Old bitch! Old bitch! There lives the mad witch!'" She looked away wearily from Dr Loneregan and gazed intently at the dusty record player.

"These days, without 'La Traviata' I have nothing to live for anymore," and she chased the pecking hens from the kitchen.

"Many years ago, Betty, you will remember me introducing you to young Guard Daly after Mass. I'm not a matchmaker, just a simple country doctor. I have cared for people all of my life and I was sure that you were both made for each other." He turned away suddenly and sniffled into a crisp white linen handkerchief. "I also heard recently in the village, that Sheamus had smashed the record collection I gave you, which upset me greatly. Do you ever hear from him these days?"

"No, never, and thanks to the good Lord, Dr Loneregan, I never want to see his face again. May he rot in poverty in London," and Betty went back to the overflowing sink and filled a kettle for tea.

Dr Loneregan simply accepted the cup of tea and drank it quickly before resuming their chat.

"I'm an old man now, Betty, but you are still a woman in the prime of life. Living alone out here can't be good for you." He carefully checked his watch. "As a member of the medical profession, I have no time or any desire for gossip, but I want you to know the following," and he looked into her smeared face and dishevelled hair. "Guard Daly was killed in a car crash last evening in Limerick," and he stopped talking while Betty blessed herself.

"God rest his young soul. He never married and I suppose you could say he was not the marrying sort. Your letter Betty never reached him at Mrs Broderick's you see. I discovered only by chance, a few days ago that Sheamus had thrown it in the river. Your brother, by all accounts, discarded everything that was good in that river. May God forgive him his sins."

Dr Loneregan got up wearily to go and Betty took his cup and saucer and saw him out to his car. "Betty, while I remember, they have started to build a small complex of nice flats in the village. Would you ever consider moving?"

"No, thank you, Dr Loneregan. It's very kind of you but this is my home until the day I die." She waved him off with more haste than was necessary and went back inside to listen again to 'La Traviata', this time at full volume. Even the hens kept their distance from the front door. Betty went into the parlour and removed an old Jacob's biscuit tin from the sideboard. Inside were large wads of twenty-pound notes in sterling; all still in pristine condition. She smiled and gently touched the top notes, happy in the knowledge that, the sum was ten thousand pounds.

Sheamus had planned to take their life savings to London from the village post office. A chance remark had revealed his crafty plan to Betty. While Sheamus slept, the night before his ferry, Betty very carefully replaced the wads of notes with exact replica sized wads of cut newspaper. She had then very cautiously put the large brown paper envelope in the exact spot under a bulky jumper in his suitcase.

Betty went over to the record player and put the scratched record on again. She gently shooed the hens from the kitchen and went out to sit on an old milk churn in the overgrown garden while still carrying the biscuit tin. In the morning she decided that she would ask Mrs O'Leary's daughter to help her clean the house and then she hoped that their eldest son Noel would drive her to Cork to buy new curtains and bits of furniture and paintings. She would even treat herself to a brand-new stereo system that, she had seen advertised in the Sunday newspapers. A complete selection of operas was added to her shopping list. Noel had offered her a sheepdog pup the previous week, but she had initially refused. Now was also the time she decided to, finally, replace poor Rover.

That night, Betty looked in the mirror again and brushed her snow-white hair with the fervour of a woman preparing for a dance in the Dooneen village hall. Her blue eyes had a new lease of life and they sparkled like Church candles in the fading evening light.

Lunch Without Laughter

Her husband's crowded funeral was jolly good fun. Sally had turned sixty a few days earlier and she murmured, "Freedom at long last," and smiled at her tearful son, Nicholas, sitting to her left in the front pew. The old Vicar's glance from the altar lingered in the air. As if declaring that, her surge of happiness was forbidden; or at the very least, inappropriate. He had droned on and on about how perfect Peter had been in the small parish of Great Smethurst. Peter's popularity as the village GP was obvious from the packed Church, but he had been a less than perfect husband. Sally and Nicholas, now at nineteen, shared this dark secret.

She grinned at Nicholas from behind the 'Order of Service' as Miss Myfanway Brockenhurst read loudly and rather condescendingly a personal eulogy for the departed. Her heavily painted black eye lashes moved erratically whenever she reached a particularly sad word or sentence. She kept looking down at Peter's oak coffin, almost willing him back to life.

"Seventy was far too young to die," she gushed; well, it would be at her age. She was a rare breed; a spinster at eighty-six. Still, she was the proud owner of seven cats and the village Church's sole organist.

Sally held Nicholas tightly by the hand; she hated seeing him cry, but his father was dead after all. A sudden heart attack on one of his early morning runs ended his life swiftly. She knew that he would have been delighted to die in his tracksuit, and that, was how he now lay athletically in the coffin. Nicholas grinned at her through shiny tears when Myfanway ended by saying rather mournfully, that Doctor Sutton had always cured her many ailments. They both smiled in unison knowing that Myfanway was a notorious village hypochondriac. The congregation stood as Myfanway made her way slowly back to the Church organ. Sally and Nicholas giggled knowingly, and the Vicar glared at them over his gold half-moon spectacles. Strains of music filled the Church and shafts of late spring sunshine struck the varnished coffin and altar almost as a rehearsed finale to life. Sally simply wanted it all to end so that, she could get on with her new life.

The cremation was a private family affair, just Sally, Nicholas, and Peter's sister Vera, whom she detested. They shared the same black limousine and she waved at the long line of mournful faces, as they pulled carefully away from the Church Yard. Vera hissed from under her black veil,

"One is not meant to indulge in waving at a funeral, Sally. Think of Peter's standing!" Nicholas retorted quite angrily: "Mum can do as she jolly well pleases, Aunt Vera. So please, shut up!"

Sally was initially unable to enter the small crematorium due to a sudden fit of laughter. Nicholas and Aunt Vera looked on in silence. When the pale, sullen faced Vicar approached the car, her laughter increased in volume.

"Oh dear! Oh dear! It's the aftershock. She will need a strong sedative," he uttered to no one in particular. Aunt Vera began to rummage in her bulky handbag for lozenges.

"I find that a lozenge, Vicar, always does the trick," and she smiled smugly at Sally.

"A lozenge, Vera, is the very last thing I need," and Sally began to dab her eyes with a tissue. "It's just something, that batty Myfanway said in Church that, has got me going. Peter would definitely understand my laughter. So sorry, Vicar, let's get it over and done with, shall we?"

Nicholas held her arm gently and they entered the desolate crematorium. Aunt Vera sat stiffly beside them and sobbed incessantly into a bright pink and not very clean handkerchief. Nicholas touched her narrow, sparrow like shoulder softly as a feeble form of apology, but she immediately shrugged him off.

As soon as Mozart's 'Laudate Dominum' began to play over the speakers, they stood and watched the coffin begin its protracted journey towards the slowly parting silk curtains. Sally and Nicholas clutched each other tightly knowing that, Peter, in his blue tracksuit and new trainers, was now within seconds of turning into white ash. The haunting music eased their final moment of turmoil, but Aunt Vera stood motionless and expressionless. The Vicar's blinking green eyes followed the coffin until the curtains closed. Then, he shut his prayer book and made an awkward bow. Aunt Vera blessed herself and began to noisily unwrap a lozenge.

Once Aunt Vera had been dropped at Morpeth railway station, they smiled with relief, as the thin black clad figure walked towards the southbound platform. She never once looked back at the car.

A month later, Sally and Nicholas drove to Reeth village in North Yorkshire with Peter's ashes in the back seat of her BMW. It was a very sunny, cheerful morning in late May, and she played Classic FM loudly. Nicholas stared ahead in a dark mood because he had wanted to drive. The house had taken on a strange, empty atmosphere without Peter, but both were still in denial. Neither of them spoke until they were on the outskirts of Reeth on a rather twisty, narrow road across the barren moor, a few miles from Leyburn. It looked and still felt decidedly chilly, even in late spring.

Nicholas grabbed his rucksack from the boot and placed the small wooden cask inside. He checked the crumpled map, and they began the trek up to the spot near a tin mine, which his dad had selected to be his final resting place. They greeted two walkers while they climbed up towards the long circular ridge outside Reeth. Sally stopped to catch her breath and admonished Nicholas for his fast-walking pace. They sat on a bed of purple heather and shared a bottle of water while admiring the stunning view of the fragmented village below. Sally had to admit that it was a perfect place.

Peter always had very good taste. He strenuously believed in physical fitness, and on the rare occasions when he had spoken of his work at dinner, it was seen as the best cure for many of his patient's ailments. Sally smiled and gazed vacantly at grazing sheep and cattle nearby and heard Peter's dulcet tones: "A bracing walk and a stiff gin and tonic usually works wonders! But all they want is pills these days!"

Peter's favourite pub and place to stay was the 'Pig & Whistle', overlooking Reeth village green. He and his old pals from medical school went there for a long weekend of walking almost every autumn. The original ten had been reduced to four or five, but Reeth remained their most popular destination.

Sally and Nicholas entered the homely pub restaurant and were shown to a table near a crackling log fire by a brisk, well-dressed lady, whom they supposed was the landlady. Their drinks were served immediately, and she cheerfully suggested the black board specials for lunch. Otherwise, she made no further fuss and went back to serve two local men at the attractive, and well-lit bar. Sally liked the woman and immediately felt at ease. It was quite a modern interior and the whitewashed walls were covered with black and white photographs showing various groups of walkers. The heat from the fireplace caused lilies in a nearby vase to fill the air with an optimistic scent.

"I like it here a lot, Mum," and Nicholas wandered over to take a closer look at the wall photographs.

After an impressive lunch they chatted earnestly over coffee and Nicholas admitted that he wanted to take a gap year with Lizzie, his girlfriend before starting University. She felt very proud to hear that, he still wanted to study medicine. *So very like his dad*, she thought and patted his short, blonde hair gently. She was not particularly keen on Lizzie who looked over painted and under nourished. Nicholas could do so much better she mused and asked the landlady for their bill. She promised to return for lunch before the end of summer.

"There's a photograph of Dad on the wall," said Nicholas excitedly as they prepared to leave, and he pointed to a small corner photograph on the back wall.

"Really? Let me see," said Sally and she went over to take a closer look. Nicholas stood behind her and teasingly showed her the crowded scene. At a small corner table sat Peter, dining with a young man, possibly not much older than Nicholas. Sally was intrigued, and asked the landlady if she knew who the young man was? After peering at the photograph, she turned and said,

"Yes, that's Mark Hudson, one of the trainee jockeys from Middleham. He's one of Lady Petronella Doyle's staff, but he's not been in for a few months. Mark is lots of fun and a great jockey by all accounts," and she smiled before putting some more logs on the fire. She turned and said, "Mark is a strong, handsome lad but has a passion for exaggeration!"

"Is Middleham nearby?" asked Sally.

"Not too far, possibly half an hour or so away," and she excused herself and went back to the bar to attend to a waiting customer. They drove in silence until Nicholas turned the car on to the A1 motorway. Sally looked across at him and said,

"I have been thinking, Nicholas, about your dad and that young man in the photograph. I just want to know more. They looked so happy together. A bit like a first date," and she laughed nervously.

"I know exactly what you are thinking, Mum. Just drive to Middleham one day. I'm very happy to go with you."

"Watch the road, please, Nicholas," said Sally sharply. "Yes, I will go back, but I need to go alone. Please understand."

By the time they reached home, neither the photograph nor for that matter, Middleham village were mentioned again.

In early September, Sally decided after carefully researching Lady Petronella Doyle's stables on the Internet that, she would telephone to see if Mark Hudson still worked at her yard. Once this was confirmed with a very polite member of staff; Sally began her journey back to North Yorkshire.

Nicholas was down in London with Lizzie, so she felt no need to tell him about the trip. It was only as she entered the long, narrow village of Middleham, that the adventure struck her as eccentric at the very least. She had been haunted by the photograph, a bit like seeing a mystery guest in a wedding photograph, whom years later makes you wonder.

It was a clear, chilly Friday morning and the view down to the gallops, which resembled a strip of airfield runway, was Yorkshire countryside at its very best. Sally stood gulping in the fresh air when a black range rover braked to a halt. The driver was a tall, elegant, grey-haired lady with a ruddy, but very fine complexion.

"Good morning. May I help you?" and Sally thought what good luck to have possibly met Lady Petronella.

"Yes, thank you. I wondered, if it might be possible to meet Mark Hudson? He was a friend of my dead husband," and she glanced at a returning line of steaming racehorses and young jockeys going into the yard.

"I'm so sorry, Sally Walker. How do you do?"

"Petronella Doyle, jolly nice to meet you. Let's go and find Mark for you," and she abandoned the car and walked Sally briskly into a large, cluttered office at the side of a row of tidy stables. A roar across the yard summoned Mark to the office within minutes. A lithe, floppy haired young man with intense blue eyes and a ready smile rushed in panting:

"You called Lady Petronella?"

"You have a visitor, Mark. Goodbye, Mrs Walker," and she closed the office door before screaming at a young stable hand mucking out nearby. Mark stood by the desk looking awkward, but then raised a neatly trimmed black eyebrow and smiled.

"You have met the boss, Lady Petronella! She's a real lady, but mad as a ship's cat."

"Yes, thank you, she's very jolly. My name is Sally Walker," and she held out her hand. "I believe you once knew my dead husband, Doctor Peter Walker." Mark sat on the edge of the desk looking visibly shaken.

"Yes, Peter, of course. I first got to know him through his shares in one of the boss's best racehorses 'The Rascal Monk'. I rode him for over three seasons, but last year, he broke a leg at Cheltenham. Had to be put down," and he looked tearfully out of the small window into the noisy, industrious yard.

Sally did not imagine that her invitation to lunch at the 'Pig & Whistle' would be accepted, but Mark rushed out to speak to the boss and Sally obediently followed him in the range rover back to Reeth. Her head was awash with questions, but by the time they had sat down in the empty restaurant, she felt foolish and vulnerable. Nicholas should definitely be here, she thought. Mark joked and teased the landlady when they placed their orders, but once she had left, the silence was ominous. After a few mouthfuls of her starter, Sally stared into Mark's eyes and said,

"Forgive me for being so forward with a stranger. Have you ever slept with my husband?" She pointed to the photographs on the nearby wall before realising that, the small black and white photograph was missing; just a solitary brass picture hook remained. Mark frowned, but said nothing, except to continue eating his soup.

"Is that why you invited me to lunch? We are total strangers," and he began to chew a chunk of bread hungrily.

"My husband was a good man Mark, and a very caring village doctor. He was by no means a perfect human being, and he had his secret side," she sighed. "He's dead now and my son Nicholas and I are the ones left wondering. I'm simply trying to fit some missing jigsaw pieces back into the puzzle. Will you help me, please?"

Mark reached out and touched her hand, very softly.

"Forgive me, Mrs Walker, for being such an ungrateful brute and lunch guest. This is not the real me, I promise you." He poured her some mineral water. "I usually laugh and joke all the time, but not today."

"Then, let's call it lunch without laughter! Much easier for us both that way," and her eyes strayed back to the gap on the wall. They ate their main courses in silence, but Sally oddly felt at ease with Mark. He had such good manners and she now wanted Nicholas to meet him more than ever. The landlady brought coffee and Sally asked her to charge the lunch bill to her room. Mark nodded and thanked her for lunch.

"Yes, Mrs Walker, there are things, that I feel I need to tell you about Peter and I." He looked at his watch. "But I must get back to the yard by five at the latest." Sally smiled and chewed one of the quirky mints left with the bill.

"Yes, of course, I do understand." She stood up and went across to double check the display of photographs. Mark noticed and said, "I know exactly what you are looking for Mrs Walker. I can explain that too," and he grinned and allowed his long fingers to pass slowly through his wavy, black hair.

"We should talk in the privacy of my room," whispered Sally hoarsely and Mark followed her upstairs. The landlady watched them and smiled as she poured a pint of bitter. Sally fumbled with the heavy room key, and Mark casually remarked, "This feels totally weird, but number four is the very same room, that I last shared here with Peter."

The Book Club

Travis hated all books and usually threw most of the paperbacks his parents gave him as encouraging presents in the dustbin. At just sixteen, he was rude, spoilt, lacking in good manners and social graces. He did badly at school and his few friends usually came from the wrong side of town.

1976 was proving to be a very long, hot summer and his father, Bob, told Travis, that he must get a job. Bournemouth was basking in welcome July sunshine when Travis approached the timbered office of the beach 'Deck Chair Manager'. Bob had confidence, that Mr Purvis, a retired Army Sergeant, may yet be the making of young Travis. Already ten minutes late, Travis sauntered into the small, very neat and organised office without as much as knocking.

"Get out, and come into my office properly, young man," shouted a 'parade square voice' from behind a rustling newspaper. Travis was stunned and jumped back on to the sun-baked pier pathway. When the newspaper was lowered, Travis was confronted by a balding, heavy-set man of middle years. His copper-coloured complexion and yellowing long sideburns indicating summer seasons spent working on the beach. He wore a smart red check shirt and a pair of baggy sandstone shorts with sharp creases. His powerful trunk-like legs were protected from the burning coarse sand by highly polished brown leather sandals. He pointed angrily at his watch and shouted: "Over ten minutes late, lad! No manners, young man. I'm already beginning to dislike you. Are you sure that, Travis Brown is your real name?"

"Yes. I'm Travis Brown," and he began to visibly shake.

"Sir! When I ask you a question or give you a job to do, I expect to hear the word 'sir'. Understood lad?"

"Yes, sir," stammered Travis and his face went bright red.

"Go back home, get yourself a T-shirt, shorts and sandals, and your trial shift starts at noon and doesn't end until every deck chair is thoroughly cleaned and stacked in the shed," and he pointed the stump of a finger in the direction of a Nissen type hut. "I will give you a week's trial. You will work closely with Adam over there. He's in charge of all ticket sales. No fairy sun lotions or sunglasses allowed either son. Am I clearly understood?" and he folded the newspaper neatly and stuck it in the top drawer of his small desk.

"Yes, sir," and Travis rushed off to collect his bike. He had never before been spoken to like that, and he sulked all the way home. But he badly needed the pocket money to save a deposit for a new chopper bike.

He was often ashamed of the old Raleigh bicycle his father had bought him.

Money was never plentiful at home and his mum couldn't work due to increasing bouts of depression. Travis was an only child, whose selfishness visibly increased with each passing year. His father did nothing but openly despair. Mr Purvis was, therefore, seen as a possible saviour.

Travis spent the very hot afternoon helping Adam and watching carefully how he operated their lengthy patch of beach. The sun was relentless, and at regular intervals, Adam cupped seawater in his large hands and splashed a cool cascade over his deeply bronzed face. He pointed towards the office where Mr Purvis surveyed the area through glinting binoculars. Adam gave Travis a friendly nudge and said, "Always remember that the Sergeant Major is closely watching how we work!"

The canvas deck chairs were rented hourly and also by the day, and Adam asked Travis to go and check the far end of their trading patch of beach. He had to hand in his takings to Mr Purvis on the hour. One middle-aged man, dozing with a white handkerchief over his face suddenly woke, making spluttering sounds. He refused to show Travis his ticket, telling him aggressively to fuck off! His large white belly looked dangerously red and his rolled up trouser legs revealed lily white and very shiny skin. *A mad Londoner* thought Travis and he scurried off to a friendly family nearby. While he carefully checked their numbered tickets and then circled the time in blue biro, the little boy threw a bucket of seawater over Travis. It felt so refreshing, and he patted the small boy and tousled his curly blond hair.

By the end of his first tiring day, Travis had grown to like Adam, more than he cared to admit, who was about three or four years older. He was tall, athletic and very good-looking and he offered the pretty sun-tanned girls on the beach free deck chairs.

"The chicks love me!" said Adam with a wink and a grin. "And the old bastard in the office will never guess that I cheat."

Travis was also full of admiration for the apparent fearlessness of his new friend. The cooling sand emitted a very strong smell of coconut suntan oil and the glowing fireball of the sun was sinking on the horizon, while both boys collected and carefully cleaned the last of the stray deck chairs. The 'Purvis Brush' was introduced by Adam and was strictly used to clean all two hundred and four deck chairs; it made their job much easier and reached every nook and cranny.

"Old Purvis designed it by all accounts for cleaning SLR rifles," said Adam with a laugh.

Mr Purvis was hunched over his desk counting coins when they knocked on his office door. He did not look up, but the spectacles on the end of his long, red nose made him a little less scary. Energetic sounds from a tennis match at Wimbledon emanated from a small black transistor radio on the edge of the desk. He ignored Travis, but had a few friendly words for Adam:

"Young Adam, that tennis match is not going well for me. Don't tell Mrs Purvis whatever you do," and he increased the volume as a particular volley between Bjorn Borg and Ilie Nastase was reaching an exciting conclusion. "I may very soon have lost a small fortune. Have put a fiver on Nastase to win!" and he spat angrily towards the radio.

Adam rode part of the way home with Travis before taking a detour to meet one of his beach chicks from nearby Christchurch. He turned and shouted: "Be smart and on time in the morning mate. Old Purvis will be very bad tempered after losing so much money on the tennis."

By late August, the intense summer sunshine still showed no signs of abating, and Mr Purvis declared that 1976 was going to be a bumper year for his business. Travis continued to work hard and had accepted that, Adam was the 'golden boy' with old Purvis. Adam was proud of his young apprentice; his sulkiness had disappeared and his friendly, respectful tone on the beach was now earning him good tips.

One of Adam's regular tricks was to politely say: "Sorry, sir, I need to go back to the office for more change. I'll return with your ten or twenty pence in a few minutes." The usual response was: "Just keep it, son."

Mr Purvis was very mean with the boy's wages, knowing full well they earned tips. But, at the end of the summer season, he was likely to pay a bonus. Adam was due to leave in early September to join the Army. His dream was to become a fully trained infantryman and to travel the world. Old Purvis was overjoyed and kept reminding Adam that he would be a Lance Corporal by the summer of 1978. "Don't forget to read lots of books, Adam. They are a sure lifeline to better and greater things, but I bet Travis never reads books!"

The boys stood in the welcome shade of the pristine office and Mr Purvis pointed excitedly to his heavy shelf of neatly arranged paperback books. Travis said nothing, but basked in the glory of hearing old Purvis using his Christian name for the first time all summer. Adam folded his arms, rocked from foot to foot, and kept smiling, knowing that, behind the books was a secret stock of small bottles of

Grecian hair tonic. He had once caught old Purvis rubbing the tonic vigorously into his trimmed sideburns, and which he claimed killed off his grey hair. Its medicinal smell lingered in the dusty air. "Don't tell a soul, Adam. Your end of season bonus will reflect our secret!" Adam had almost forgotten the concealed bottles until now.

Mr Purvis took a book down very carefully and showed the boys the faded front cover: A Tale of two Cities. "Who wrote this wonderful book, lads?" and he placed it cover side down by his heavy cash box. "The great man, Charles Dickens, you simpletons," he growled and wiped a bead of sweat from his greasy forehead.

"I bet neither one of you has ever heard of Chekhov?" Before the boys got a chance to answer, he proudly retorted: "Chekhov saved my marriage, I'll have you know. You ask Daphne when she's next down at the beach giving us her delicious madeira cake."

Adam kept staring at Mr Purvis knowing that, Daphne, in her billowing floral dresses, rarely put in an appearance at the hut, or the beach. He remembered her visit at the start of the season. A large, unsmiling woman with extra thick spectacles and the pallor of a prisoner was his recollection.

"I will certainly ask her Mr Purvis," uttered a bemused Adam and Travis looked on in a bewildered fashion. Mr Purvis returned both books cautiously and neither boy got a chance to even see what this man, Chekhov, had actually written. He then sat back at his desk and folded his hairy arms. "Boys, it's almost the end of the season, and as I'm in a pretty good mood, I shall let you into a little secret!" and he gently tapped the right side of his large, peeling nose. "You are in the esteemed presence of the President of the

Boscombe Book Club, no less," and he rubbed his hands gleefully together. Adam looked across at Travis and both boys kept staring at Mr Purvis nervously. They had never seen him in such a good mood, and it was slightly worrying that, he may just have gone mad before paying them their summer bonus.

"We had better be off, Mr Purvis," said Adam earnestly. "It's already gone seven and Travis and me still have loads of deckchairs to clean and stack." Mr Purvis kept staring out the office door at the relatively calm blue sea. "I've often wondered boys what it would be like to swim like a dolphin under those waves. Amazing, don't you think?" He looked back slowly at his heaving shelf of books and smiled before choosing a further two books. He shook his head sadly and turned his gaze back out to sea. "Daphne hates the sea. She can't swim you see," and he leant and slightly adjusted one of the books on his desk. "Daphne always says: 'Nothing is ever like it appears on the surface.' She's usually right, you know, lads."

The boys left old Purvis nodding and grinning to himself and got to work on the remaining empty deckchairs. He didn't appear to notice their sudden departure and he continued to talk to himself from behind the highly polished desktop. Then, a few minutes later, a shout reverberated across the beach summoning them for their bonus. At that moment, Adam and Travis stopped stacking the deckchairs, which still retained a certain degree of warmth from the day's glorious sunshine. Adam threw his arm over Travis's sun burned shoulder and they walked slowly up the beach, no longer in fear of old Purvis and his office rituals. But knowing that, summer was about to end, and their close bond of friendship would shortly be broken. Travis felt tears welling in his eyes and blamed the stiff sea breeze.

Bed 7

Mrs Winifred Hopkins sat comfortably on a faded picnic rug, which she had struggled to place down on the uneven bed of rocks, due to an unseasonably brisk sea breeze. The red tartan pattern of the rug took on a new lease of life in the bright July sunshine. This was her 'reserved spot' in the rugged bay with Staithes as a majestic old-world backdrop and the ruffled sea enabling her to relax and dream without barriers.

She dipped her pale white feet in a little rock pool and smiled at the sudden tingling sensation through her old toes. It was the first time she had removed her nylon stockings out of doors that year. Seagulls nearby, dipped in flight and squawked, but these familiar sounds reminded her of happy summer holidays spent with her husband, Donald, and their two girls, Mavis and Brenda in this exact same place. Winifred closed her eyes and heard the girls squealing with delight as they lowered their tiny fishing nets into the surprising depths of the many paddling pools. Donald always stretched, snoring under a folded newspaper, and still dressed in long black trousers and a short-sleeved shirt: his only casual concession to mark the arrival of summer.

She took a packet of ginger nut biscuits from her tidy canvas shopping bag and nibbled the hard biscuit base trying to avoid dislodging her ill-fitting dentures. The sunshine warmed her now well-worn face and she adjusted the brim of her straw hat; her mottled skin no longer reacted well to the strong sun. Winifred blinked through thick spectacles and watched a young family swimming in the bay. The little, darkly tanned girl using a blue and yellow rubber swimming ring sounded just like Brenda. *Those were such happy days*, thought Winifred, taking another ginger nut from the packet. The day trip was exactly what she needed, even though she was alone. Mavis was living in New Zealand, but at least Brenda was in Harrogate. Both girls, now well into their fifties, never made much fuss of their mother who was rapidly approaching her eightieth birthday. Donald died over twenty years ago, and these days she had some difficulty remembering what he even looked like.

Staithes, reliably, brought her family back to life and she cherished the good memories, and was equally careful to avoid the bad ones. Neither of her girls had married and this troubled Winifred. She liked to think that, when she was gone, they would not grow old without experiencing the love of a good man. Donald had been a good man, but he hid his other side. Her girls deserved better.

Winifred dozed off when the sun was shrouded by a patch of peculiar fluffy shaped clouds. She took off her hat and pushed her feet deeper into the little pillow of sand. A scampering baby crab tickled her toes, and she took a deep breath of salty air to savour that, long forgotten sensation. Being at the seaside made her feel hungry and she disturbed her carefully folded nylons to remove a tinfoil package of cheese and pickle sandwiches. She munched each one with great pleasure and even threw the odd crust to the frantic seagulls. Two rather large birds dived with precision into the surf and gobbled the floating soggy white bread.

She noticed the family nearby were already packing up their things, so she checked her watch. The bus was not due to leave for a further two hours, so she replaced her straw hat and lay back against the small indent of warm rocks. By closing her eyes, she intensified the peace and intermittent sounds and seaweed smells from the sun-drenched bay.

The sun lost none of its ferocity, and there was a late afternoon heat haze over the sea while Winifred gathered her things. She decided to be daring and to travel home without wearing nylons. She quickly and surreptitiously rinsed her dentures in the seawater; the salty taste made her gasp, but she celebrated being naughty, by chuckling to herself on the narrow path by the cliffs. She held on to her straw hat in the buffeting wind.

Winifred picked a window seat, mid-way down the bus and watched the other passengers boarding. She celebrated their happy, healthy looks until a dark-haired young woman sat in the opposite row. She smiled and nodded in Winifred's direction, but the right side of her face was very badly disfigured. Winifred blinked and took a deep breath. The burn scars took her straight back to Christmas Day 1959 and Brenda's accident.

Donald's potatoes on Christmas Day had to be just right. Golden, crispy balls of flavour after being roasted in goose fat and fresh thyme from their village back garden. Winifred caught the handle of the old roasting tin in her apron waist string spilling the spluttering contents into the watchful, innocent gaze of small Brenda. Her screams and the way the skin melted and just fell away, caused Winifred to freeze on the spot; she felt a shiver travel down her spine and reached for a handkerchief to wipe her brow.

The young woman was still smiling and offered her some crisps from a rustling orange bag. She accepted gladly and thought that Brenda's facial scars were far worse. The Consultant had told them back then that, the years would be kind to her injuries. He was wrong of course, but his words at that, awful time were like sweet notes of music to Donald and Winifred. Donald always blamed her and went to his grave bearing a deep grudge at her stupidity. She bore his grudge with a sort of wise humility, but thankfully Brenda had loved them both with equal fervour. Up until his death, Donald steadfastly refused roast potatoes every Christmas Day as a mark of respect for his unfairly disfigured daughter.

Mavis was her father's pet and bore a silent hostility towards her mother. She was the less pretty one and she sometimes poked fun at her sister's scarring. She once said: 'You have a map of Italy on your cheek,' before bursting into tears and running away from the dinner table. Winifred always blamed herself for causing Mavis to emigrate to New Zealand. She was doing well as a highly paid mid-wife, but her life in coloured photographs appeared somehow hollow and empty to her mother. She finished eating her crisps and wiped the light film of grease from her lips.

The young woman was chatting to a youth behind her but had turned the good side of her face towards him. Winifred started to cry and dabbed her eyes with her wrinkled handkerchief. She soon nodded off, and the bus was on the outskirts of a cloudy Harrogate when the chatter from the remaining passengers woke her. The seat felt cold, and she had an urge to replace her nylons. Staithes was by now a distant, sun filled pool of memories.

"You had a bad fall, Mother, stepping off the bus:" Winifred could hear these floating words from Brenda who clasped her hand as she lay rigidly in Bed 7 at The County Hospital. "You have been here for almost a week, Mother. The nurses are wonderful," and she smiled half-heartedly in the general direction of quite a stern looking uniformed figure trying to prop up an old lady in a nearby bed.

"Good care and good food, and we'll have you back home in no time."

"I don't think so Brenda. This is the end of the road for me. I know it," mumbled Winifred before looking away.

"Don't be so ridiculous, Mother. You had a serious fall, that's all there is to it." Brenda could feel her normal irritation building up again and she removed her right hand from the cold pale skin of her mother's furrowed brow.

"Stop all that mumbling, Mother. Where are your dentures?"

"They took them away, yesterday," and she started to sob. Brenda knelt down on the cold floor and rummaged in the small bedside locker. At the back were her mother's dentures wrapped in a sticky, phlegm-stained handkerchief. When she unfolded the sour smelling cloth, a few grains of Staithes sand trickled on to the floor. Brenda went off to complain to the Duty Sister and then rinsed her mother's stained yellow teeth in the toilet sink. Once Winifred had regained her dignity, Brenda saw that, the old fighting spirit was returning to her mother. She smiled and asked chirpily for tea and a digestive biscuit.

"I don't like her one bit. She can't be trusted, Brenda." And she pointed at the same stern looking figure who was now distributing medication from a rattling trolley. "Molly in that corner bed hates her too. She loudly calls her Hitler!"

"You and Molly are simply tired and confused, that's all. No one here is going to harm you. Maybe your medication is too strong. I shall have words with the Duty Sister on the way out," and she took the empty cup and saucer from her frail, trembling hands.

"Please don't complain to any of them nurses, Brenda. Once you have left, they will take it out on all of us in the ward. Mark my words, I'm scared in here." And she closed her eyes, uttering a deep sigh of despair. Brenda had never before seen her mother in such a state and blamed the unfamiliar hospital surroundings. But, the cold, almost uncaring tone of the sister at the nursing station lingered in her mind. On the way out, she decided to remain silent and bade a cheerful farewell to the duty nursing staff. A small, foreign looking woman pushing the tea trolley smiled and waved and said, "God bless." The others resembled unsmiling waxwork dummies and she worried about her mother and Molly on the drive home.

At the end of a long telephone call to Mavis in New Zealand, she decided to mention her concern about some of the nursing staff. Mavis was her usual cold self and said that they were both being delirious. After replacing the receiver, Brenda shed tears of despair. She told herself to keep strong, as Mother needed her now more than ever. She busied herself making tea, determined not to give in to another bout of depression. Mavis had sounded like a stranger on the telephone, and she reflected upon this all evening. There was one snippet of conversation that, haunted her while she attempted to watch the late news – 'She shouted that, I might choke on my dentures, Brenda. Have you ever heard such rot? Experts on everything in life, except life itself!' She would have to get her mother out of there somehow, before it was too late. The hollow cheeks, sunken eyes and unwashed, greasy grey hair was more than she could bear. Bed 7 had suddenly become a gateway to her mother's grave. That night, Brenda sensed that, her scarring had begun to tingle again, and she cried herself softly to sleep.

The rain fell with a tropical ferocity and the street drain near 'Bettys Tea Shop' in Harrogate was foaming and gurgling like some strange sea creature about to emerge from the deep. It was just over a month since her mother had died suddenly in Bed 7. According to Molly's daughter, Marilyn, she was the fifth person to die in that, particular bed in the last six months. Brenda took shelter in the grand entrance to Betty's and watched the cheerful bustle of people buying freshly baked bread and intrinsically decorated cakes. Even the smells were intoxicating and uplifting, and she began to emerge ever so slightly from the dark place she had occupied since the funeral. She was deep in thought when a dishevelled, tall figure entered and shook her umbrella vigorously on the entrance tiles.

Marilyn was a similar age to Brenda and they both shared she imagined the same doubts about two of the nurses. Molly was now safely back at her farmhouse and had recalled some dreadful stories about the ward. The two ladies ordered the special afternoon tea and initially had a gossip to relieve the tension and Brenda's heartbreak at the untimely death of her mother. Mavis never came back for the funeral, and her 'work commitments' had sounded hollow on the telephone. Marilyn had already recruited a close friend she said to work 'under cover' at the Hospital.

Brenda was simply unable to contain her tears.

"I'm so sorry. They are all looking at us, Marilyn," said a hoarse sounding Brenda.

"Think nothing of it, my dear. Just imagine, that, within a few weeks, the mystery of Bed 7 will have been solved. No one else deserves to suffer such a fate," and she patted Brenda's jam-stained hand. Brenda's face suddenly brightened, and she felt a surge of optimism return. Strawberry jam had never tasted as good as this. She studied the delicate workings of Marilyn's gloved hands with a shiny pastry fork and thought how very stylish.

"Thanks ever so much, Marilyn. I somehow know that my dear mother will finally rest in peace."

Marilyn insisted upon paying the bill, and as Brenda awkwardly kissed her farewell, she glimpsed a police car parked by the kerb side, outside Bettys Tea Shop. A policewoman approached them briskly and tapped Marilyn's shoulder firmly but calmly. Brenda stood on the pavement pale and speechless, as her friend was ushered urgently into the back seat. Marilyn gave her a sort of half wave and suddenly Brenda was alone with her thoughts. But for a split second, she could have sworn that, Marilyn was wearing her dead mother's wedding ring. It was the familiar way the stone glinted when she waved.

"Oh my God!" she screamed before collapsing heavily on the wet shiny pavement.

The Tea Dancers

I'm an overweight widower with a pacemaker, and my name is Billy O'Leary. I no longer shower or shave for that matter, every morning. There's no point really; well not since my darling wife, Mary, died on a glorious sunny day in early May 1996.

I remember the gin clear sky and the drifting birdsong that warm morning, as if it was yesterday. Ten long years have already passed without her eager smile and the great smells that, escaped from our farmhouse kitchen. She truly loved me; our two border collies, Shep and Nell, and nothing ever seemed to bother the woman. We married in our late teens, but never had any children. That caused Mary a great deal of pain, yet she bore her sadness with tremendous grace. She quickly understood that I was not good in that department; the subject was taboo back then in the tiny village of Glenmaloo.

Our farm was over one hundred acres of fertile grazing land, surrounded to the West by a large lake with a rugged shoreline and a range of conifer-clad hills that, the American visitors often called mountains. Mary loved her summer dips in the cold, clear water of the lake and the picnics she carried in her neat rucksack for her ageing parents. Her father could be a difficult man, but in the end, he saw fit to pass me the farm. It was her saintly mother who convinced him that, I was not a bad man. Until the day he died, he held a stubborn grudge against me for not fathering children. He craved a grandson almost as much as his nightly tumbler of whisky. I still recall his flushed rugged cheeks being caressed by the flames from the sods of turf burning fiercely in the kitchen grate.

Mary baked soda bread and apple cakes for visitors on a Monday and a Friday afternoon. After milking our tidy herd of cows, I looked forward to stepping across the kitchen hearth. The fresh baking smells sort of kidnapped my senses, and I was sometimes rewarded with Mary creeping up behind my tired body and placing her flour-drenched hands over my eyes. Her slim figure and infectious laughter haunt me to this very day. She never complained about anything.

The farmland is now leased, and the village doctor, a kindly Dublin man, told me to get out of the house more. I don't have any hobbies, except for a spot of fishing on the lake, but at seventy-nine, I can't sit for very long on the chilly, exposed shoreline.

It was after the 7 a.m., Mass one Sunday morning that, Brigid Sheehan mentioned the 'Tea Dancers' to me. Well, sure I never connected the ample buttocks of Brigid to anything as graceful or athletic as dancing. She hated Mary (God rest her soul!) for some obscure reason and was always known as the village gossip. She had married a British soldier during the 1970s and had a young son. By all accounts, they still live somewhere in England, and Brigid works in the only pub in the village when not looking after her grumpy mother.

Brigid is no 'oil painting' these days. She can best be described as small and fat, with very manly feet. Her tight grey perm, red cheeks and thick spectacles remind me of the old-fashioned Matrons in Hospitals. She's a kind-hearted soul and I told her in the chill wind by the caravan selling those boring Church newspapers, that I would definitely think about it. She gave a sort of shrill chortle while counting coins to purchase some Catholic Herald or other.

The 'thinking about it' took almost six months. Then, on a sunny Wednesday afternoon in May, I stepped into the farmyard in my best tweed sports jacket and brown trousers with a strong set of braces. I had washed properly and shaved my face in the cracked mirror with extra care, and even splashed some of the aftershave that Mary had given me over twenty-five years ago. It took ages to open the bottle and the spicy smell brought tears to my sunken eyes. I put the front door key carefully under a clay barn owl on a wooden perch by the front gate and walked slowly down the lane to wait for Brigid in her black Morris Minor. A classic car that, belched exhaust fumes endlessly, and she was known as the worst driver in Glenmaloo; an accolade she seemed to cherish with a spinsterish pride.

Billy eased himself slowly into the low passenger seat and they took off in a motion, that could best be described as more Kangaroo-like! There was a very sickly smell of cheap perfume, so Billy wound down the window, only to be glared at by Brigid. An extremely tight manoeuvre followed to avoid death from an oncoming speeding tractor.

"That fool Shaun Herlihy needs some driving lessons," screamed Brigid and she waved her fist at him. Shaun looked to be in some sort of rural trance, and he clipped off a large chunk of hedgerow, which bounced along the narrow road like some oversized football.

"It runs in the family, Billy. His father was a simpleton. A forced marriage, I can tell you. Always the worst," and she rummaged in the teak dashboard and offered Billy a fruit pastille from a dirty looking mangled paper roll. He smiled and quietly chewed the pastille while they sped past the sprawling Herlihy farmstead.

"I knew his mother, Betty, well," said Billy, purely for something to say and to take his mind off her awful driving. The pub carpark was already full, but Brigid reversed at unnecessary speed into a muddy corner. Billy was then obliged to get out of the car through the driver's door and he experienced a sharp shot of pain through his bad leg.

Billy held the door into 'Keefe's County' open and Brigid made one of her grand entrances. The bar was filled with swirling smoke as they passed through to the larger back lounge, which had a tidy dance floor and a raised platform for John Aherne and his best friend, Mikie Hickey. John played the violin (not very well!) and Mikie played the upright piano with a modest degree of creativity. Neither gentleman could read their music sheets; however, they were strategically placed on shiny metal stands purely for show.

A group of about twenty or so 'Tea Dancers' of all ages, shapes and sizes sat at small tables facing the musicians. Brigid knew everyone and dragged Billy around in her wake, with a flurry of hasty introductions. A slim, dark-haired woman appeared with a tray of steaming teapots, called Rosie O'Dowd. Brigid remarked before finally sitting down next to Billy, that Rosie was the vital mascot for the Tea Dancers.

"Wait till you taste one of her omelettes, Billy. I'm not a bad cook myself, as you know. But I can't compete with Rosie's omelettes. They say the knack lies in the whisking of the eggs you see..." and Brigid drank her strong tea with a slurp and a vacant look in her eyes.

John Aherne was making quite a racket tuning his violin, but no one seemed to mind, or even notice. The tea was being drunk energetically and Rosie's hot buttered scones disappeared in seconds.

"Just some nourishment before we hit the dance floor," whispered Brigid from across the table. Billy watched her swallow half a scone, and the crumbs floated down the front of her orange cardigan like the first snowflakes of winter. *By God, she's some woman*, thought Billy. He liked the way her cardigan reflected her heavily powdered cheeks, and suddenly her cheap perfume caused a stirring in his loins. He sipped his tea and tapped his feet under the table to the out of tune sounds of 'The Rose of Tralee'.

"What a ferocious noise," hissed Brigid through gritted false teeth. A stray crumb of scone flew through the air.

"Sure, I quite like the music, Brigid. It's a happy sort of sound," said a contented Billy lifting another cup of tea to his chapped lips.

"It's not the music, you clown," snapped Brigid. "It's him in the far corner," and she pointed her teacup. "That fool, Kevin Twomey slurping tea from his saucer. He still can't get used to his new set of bottom teeth. He's had them for over a year now!" And she folded her strong arms in disgust. Billy had always been fascinated by Brigid's calloused hands; in her day, God bless the woman, she could milk a herd of cows single handed in all weathers. She was not a woman to wear gloves, except of course at funerals.

"Fair dues to you, Brigid. You have a terrific pair of hands. God bless them," and he smiled in the direction of the band.

"What are you blathering about, Billy. This dancing business has made you light in the head." She stood up quickly and went over to speak sternly to Kevin Twomey. Billy kept on tapping his feet and tried to imagine waltzing close to Brigid. *Oh, that summer rose perfume*, he thought, *may go to my old head*. He looked around the lounge smiling and helped himself to Brigid's second buttered scone, feeling a light flush of youth soaring to his cheeks.

Brigid grabbed the microphone from the wobbly stand and asked the Tea Dancers to be quiet. The dancing was about to begin, and everyone was told that, they had to take the floor. There were not enough men to go around, so the ladies were told to share one man from each of the tables. She asked for raised hands for fresh omelettes, which Rosie O'Dowd would prepare during the last waltz of the afternoon. Our favourite: 'The Blue Danube' she loudly reminded her rapt audience.

"Jesus, Rosie is some woman. Can you imagine cooking thirty omelettes during a last waltz?" said Billy to the sour faced creature in black next to him. She looked right through him and clapped almost too energetically at Brigid's stilted, public announcements.

"It's always that Blue Danube. Foreign muck if you ask me!" snarled the sour faced creature.

Brigid thoroughly enjoyed the lingering applause and made quite a fuss of switching off the old microphone. She stood on the edge of the stage like some actress bidding her audience a last farewell. It all ended with a loud bang through the speakers and a worried looking John Aherne started to nervously flick an array of switches on an amplification device that, wouldn't look out of place in the local garage welding shop. Mikie Hickey struck a few chords on his piano and after a prolonged hissing sound the room was almost deafened by the volume.

"For God's sake, get going lads; it's already past four," shouted Brigid and a cloud of spittle landed on Mikie's shiny, bald, head. It was clear from her posture by the dance floor that as Secretary of 'The Tea Dancers', she was in no mood for any further delays.

The mediocre music began to float around the lounge and the sipping of tea was silenced. Couples emerged from the gloom and the dancing started with self-conscious stiffness. A mixture of smells from cheap perfumes to after-shaves, and stale sweat permeated the already stuffy air. Billy stood idly waiting for Brigid to emerge from the pub kitchen where she was placing the final omelette order with her secretarial business posture and forced efficiency. He heard a loud laugh from Rosie O'Dowd, pierce the air like a roll of thunder. Then, he was pushed roughly in the direction of the dance floor by the sour faced creature. It was only when he took her scrawny, and not very clean hand that, he noticed she was wearing wellington boots. He looked longingly at the table he had vacated and there sat a po-faced Brigid. Her strong milking fingers tapped the table with vigour, and he felt a cold shiver down his spine. One of the sour faced creature's large wellington boots caught on his shoelace and they both toppled in an untidy heap on the glossy paraffin-stained floor.

A Defaced Fiver

'Love is like water. We can fall into it, we can drown in it, but we cannot live without it.'

The Offertory Motet by Palestrina drifted robustly around the Church of the Immaculate Conception like scudding clouds on an offshore breeze. Mrs Dilys Montague-Murphy pressed her shiny white knuckles against the highly polished wood of the pew prayer book rest and closed her eyes allowing the fine music to carry her away.

Dilys, at fifty-seven was unmarried, but she used 'Mrs' with insistent joy, and ever since she had discovered those solemn Latin Masses at Farm Street, she craved acceptance from the mainly 'well heeled' parishioners. 'Her husband, who is apparently in finance, moved to Cannes with his young secretary, over five years ago. Poor Dilys, left comfortably off by all accounts,' was often whispered politely when refreshments were served after Mass.

Her 'white lie' had gained conviction and momentum ever since she attended her first Mass back in 2010. It was the last Sunday in October, to be precise, a drizzly, dreary Sunday in London. She wanted to do something quite special for her fiftieth birthday, but nothing came easily to mind. The morning was devoted to having a hot bath and drying her long grey hair with rough towels. The bathroom was shared in the shabby house in Willesden Green where she rented a small, poorly furnished room from an unsmiling Indian landlady. Dilys knew that, after thirty minutes or so, Shakira, the landlady would rattle the door handle with venom. Still, it was all she could afford. Ever since Dilys left Watergrasshill, a small nondescript Irish village, back in the early 1980s, her dreams of success and riches in London had been constantly shattered. So, her Sunday escapes by underground to elegant Mayfair and the Latin Mass, were the oxygen of a life that she still craved.

Dilys dressed plainly but smartly, and everything was sourced from Charity Shops in good parts of London. Her long, grey hair was plaited in a neat ponytail, which she was in a habit of lightly swishing whenever she solemnly approached the altar. A handsome woman with fine features and good skin; she had practiced her lowly bow to the glinting tabernacle before climbing the six wooden steps to the pulpit. Father Sweeney, the elderly parish priest liked Dilys, and her readings at Mass had become a source of mild amusement. Dilys used the pulpit for a form of elocution lesson practice, and she lingered and laboured over certain words for maximum dramatic affect. Father Sweeney appeared oblivious, but some parishioners had grown tired of her Sunday performances, and said so, but ever so politely over refreshments in the vestry.

Word had also spread that Dilys was an heiress to the Murphy stout family. She had sown that seed one Christmas Eve after a particularly bad week as a house cleaner. She had three regular homes on her cleaning books but had foolishly taken on a fourth. The rich, brash lady from New York had refused to pay Dilys shouting from the doorway that, her cleaning was crap! Those words hurt Dilys, even to this day. It was money she badly needed at the time, so she went back to cleaning the three regular homes with even greater care. She just couldn't see a way of escaping from her life of domestic drudgery, and the smiles and nods of appreciation in the vast Church were a real comfort and safe sanctuary for Dilys.

On one of her regular Sundays at Farm Street, Major Henry Warburton who helped and oversaw the small team taking the collection during Mass, failed to turn up. Dilys stood in willingly for the Major, and there was quite a considerable increase in the collection, which greatly pleased old Father Sweeney. Dilys sat comfortably at the Major's tidy, small desk and carefully counted the wide array of notes. It was while she was counting a small stack of fivers, that she suddenly noticed, that one of the notes had been defaced. A mobile telephone number was written carelessly, but legibly under the head of HM The Queen. Dilys removed it with an irritated flourish and replaced it with a note from her handbag. Some people these days have no respect or manners she muttered.

Father Sweeney escorted Lady Hamilton towards Dilys while she sipped a cup of strong tea. Dilys was no fan of the formidable Lady Arabella Hamilton, but she was keenly aware of her reputation, and legendary generosity to the Church.

"How very nice to see you, Dilys, looking so elegant and vigorous. Your readings get better every Sunday. I really don't know how you do it." Dilys forced a smile while shaking Lady Hamilton's bright pink gloved hand.

"I just feel part of the Farm Street family, Lady Hamilton."

"And so, you should, my dear. Father Sweeney would be completely lost without you."

"Quite so, your Ladyship," said the stooped figure of the elderly parish priest as he was approached by another very important parishioner.

Dilys lingered in the vestry and always helped the other volunteers with the washing up. After Sunday Mass and the vestry tea and biscuits, there was little else for Dilys to look forward to. Sometimes, she went alone to the nearby Curzon Cinema to watch a movie and chew a bag of soft centred chocolates, which rustled when she least expected the flimsy wrappers to do so. Heads usually turned, but then Dilys fresh from her performance in the pulpit, saw herself as a sort of resting actress, and ignored them. Sunday was the longest day of the week, and in winter it wore a sort of melancholic veil.

A few months passed and it was on one of her regular journeys home by tube that Dilys thought again of the defaced fiver. She very carefully removed it from her bulky handbag and began to stare at the telephone number. She was conscious that the fat, sweaty man in a tracksuit opposite was looking at her intently. *Just another London nutter,* she thought and firmly shut the brass Celtic Harps, which entwined to protect the cheap contents of her sole, black, fake leather handbag.

Dilys would love to have married a nice, plain looking man with a good job, but it never happened. She dreamt of summer holidays in Ireland with her husband by her side and two well-behaved children. Heads would turn in the small parish Church in Watergrasshill when they took their seats near the altar. It was usually at the moment when her son, Frank started crying that, she woke up feeling empty, unloved and disorientated.

Shakira was parking her small red Fiat in one of the resident's parking bays while Dilys was opening the front door. She was a very skilled city driver and while completing the final manoeuvre, the car window slid silently down. "I need to have a word, Dilys, please. Hope you have enjoyed your Sunday outing?" Dilys stood smiling and motionless and wished that, Shakira didn't call her attendance at Mass an outing. "Well, she is Indian after all, and everything is an outing for them," she muttered sharply.

Shakira opened the boot and removed a large canvas bag, which usually contained plastic boxes of different dishes made by her married daughter in Chiswick. She's either going to invite me in for a meal or to increase the rent; usually it was the latter, whenever Shakira wanted to have a word. They both removed their bulky coats in the entrance hall and Shakira looked extremely elegant in her blue and red sari. She was a good-looking woman, with very cold, empty eyes, and a temper to match. "I hope you don't mind me saying so, Dilys – you look ever so drawn and pale these days. Is everything okay?"

Dilys was quite taken aback. She was unused to such frankness as a tenant, but at least the conversation was not about the rent. She didn't want to have to move, but any increase would push her over budget in her present circumstances. If only they knew at Farm Street how badly off she really was. Her white lies haunted her, but she had no choice. Without those weekly Latin Masses, her life would be almost pointless.

"Yes, of course, Shakira. Why wouldn't it be? I'm always very busy you know and living here suits me, perfectly. It's the cold winter weather. Sure, 'tis not good for man or beast!" And she laughed nervously while stroking her shocking pink silk scarf.

"Come for supper in 'my' kitchen tomorrow evening, Dilys. I will cook a nice mild chicken curry for you with your favourite chapatti breads. Is 6 p.m., okay dear?"

Dilys hesitated before answering: "Yes of course, Shakira. That would be lovely." She climbed the stairs to her room at the ivy covered back of the house knowing that the curry and the other packed meals had already been made by Shakira's unhappily married daughter. She could hear the fridge door being opened and the familiar clatter of containers with sticky labels showing the date and type of dish. There was rarely anything in her diary, but after summoning up sufficient courage, she had finally telephoned the number on the old five-pound note. He sounded quite young, possibly foreign, but so nice and polite. She had already agreed to meet him for a drink on the same Monday evening. His name was Stefan and he told Dilys exactly what he would be wearing at the Stratton Street exit from Green Park underground station. She decided to make some excuse when she met Shakira the next morning.

For now, all of her thoughts were on Stefan and the ease with which he had asked her out. As she prepared for bed, she kept reminding herself that, it was not a 'date' in any real sense of the word. The whole thing felt curious, yet she imagined that, the discovery of the fiver in Church gave the adventure a sort of religious resonance.

Her mother's voice: "Good things happen to those who wait!" from years back offered her a source of silent, heavenly approval. It will only be a drink in a public place. "He sounds young enough to be my son" were words uttered by Dilys to console herself. She knelt down by the narrow wooden bed and prayed more fervently than she had done in years. She admitted quietly to the good Lord that, she was a lonely woman in desperate need of love and male companionship and hoped that the Lord might understand.

Shakira seemed very irritated when Dilys told her that, extra duties at Farm Street meant cancelling supper. By noon, her grey ponytail had disappeared, and she walked back to the house feeling almost lightheaded. Her new style, neatly cut hair with blond highlights caused her to stop outside Waterstones Bookshop. She saw a much younger looking stranger in the reflected glass and tilted her head sideways in the sunshine. *What will they make of me on the pulpit next Sunday*, she thought, and a worried frown made her suddenly look too mature. There was no going back now, and the forty-five pounds was money she was saving for her next visit to Ireland.

It was Stefan's manners that, impressed Dilys most, and he held the door wide open when they entered 'The Punch Bowl' on Farm Street. Some supper there was her idea, as the restaurants in this part of the city looked far too expensive. They found a small table and she ordered beers and a platter of meats for sharing. Once she had established that, none of the Church regulars were in the pub, she visibly relaxed and removed her light fawn coloured coat. His tanned skin caught the sunlight, and they quietly toasted this odd meeting. 'Cheers,' said Stefan with a big smile. Dilys almost swooned at his foreign accent and good looks. They had not spoken much on the short walk from Green Park tube station. She had felt particularly awkward being hugged on the street by such a handsome young man. He's a total stranger she thought and also far too young.

When their platter of meats arrived, she flicked her head nervously before remembering her lost ponytail. Stefan smiled and said: "I'm very happy, Dilys."

"Your wonderful accent, Stefan – where are you from exactly?" And she offered him first choice from the platter.

"I'm from Romania and here in London to study medicine. Are you by any chance a doctor? You certainly look like one, but a very beautiful doctor." Her heart missed a beat and she savoured Stefan's unexpected compliments more than their lunch.

"You are a real charmer, Stefan," and they both burst into fits of laughter. He didn't look like a trainee doctor to Dilys, but she had never known any doctors in a social sense. She felt so happy that, she wanted to believe everything he was telling her. His dark suit and open necked white shirt suggested a very good upbringing. His highly polished black shoes reminded her of Father Sweeney, who always insisted that, shoes usually told you everything you needed to know about a man.

"No, Stefan, I'm not a medical woman. I run a small business and work in St James's Church Piccadilly as a volunteer." She considered it best to be a little on her guard, as she had fallen hopelessly under his magic spell.

Dilys ordered more beers and another platter of meats noticing that the small, cosy pub was now full of regulars. She shifted uncomfortably when she saw Major Henry Warburton at the bar. He was immaculately dressed with a neatly folded Telegraph newspaper under his left arm. "Are you feeling okay, Dilys?" said Stefan gently. "Your mind seems drifting, if that is the correct English word to use?" She smiled and shook her head before making room on the cramped table for a fresh platter of meats. By now the Major was safely in a corner buried under his open newspaper. Dilys frowned wondering how she could ever explain Stefan to the Major, and she had already lied about the name of the Church. *He may not even recognise me in my new hairstyle*, she thought cheerfully, before resuming their very tasty supper. The two small beers and Stefan's presence had caused Dilys to feel a bit lightheaded. She had never done anything like this in her life and it just felt good and very exciting. Suddenly, Dilys said: "I do have a close friend called Mary Tyson, and she's a doctor. Well, a psychiatrist, but a very successful one in London. A very bright woman indeed and a regular church goer." She felt smug to have remembered Mary Tyson, who had been in reality a school bully. "I just hope she's now in prison," Dilys muttered, but then she felt slightly uncomfortable.

"London is full of mad people. So, your friend must be very rich by now," said a smiling Stefan.

"I'm not so sure of that, Stefan, she has a big family to look after," and Dilys nodded before checking on the Major. "She's a good Catholic woman, you see."

"My father back in Romania is a banker and he always says that there is much money to be made from madness! What do you think, Dilys?"

"What a strange question to ask me, Stefan. Maybe –" she paused to chew a tough slice of chorizo sausage – "you must think I'm mad to have called your number. I kept that five-pound note in my handbag, more out of curiosity than anything else."

"What would your husband think if he saw you now?" and Stefan drank the last shiny droplets of his beer.

"He's dead, Stefan. He died some years ago in Kenya from a snakebite. I would rather not talk about it just now, if you don't mind." And she used her serviette to wipe away a tear. Stefan stroked her shoulder, and she visibly shook from his strong, sensual touch. He continued to massage the back of her neck with deft fingers.

"You are far too tense, Dilys. Let Doctor Stefan relax you." He smiled and looked into her eyes. Dilys felt quite faint and was very glad to see that, the Major had already left.

"Am I correct in assuming that you don't have a man friend in your life?"

"No, I am afraid not, Stefan. I find it difficult to trust men in London."

"Such a great shame, Dilys. You are a very beautiful woman," and he stood up offering to buy more beer.

"Not for me, Stefan. I drink very little these days and I know my limits," and she picked up her half full beer glass very carefully.

Shortly after 10 p.m., they parted company at Green Park underground station. Ever the gentleman, Stefan stood waving until she disappeared into the hungry mouth of the escalator. Numbers had been exchanged and she knew they would most likely meet again. She felt deliriously happy and was still giddy with excitement when she entered the house. It was a relief to notice that Shakira was already in bed watching television.

A couple of weeks slowly passed without any word from Stefan. Then, after a particularly well received reading at the 11 a.m. Solemn Latin Mass, while helping with the teas, she heard the old mobile phone give a muffled ping in her handbag. Unable to read the text, she decided to wait until she had left the Church. It was from Stefan and the number of spelling mistakes surprised Dilys. She wondered how he could cope with his medical examinations using such poor English. But it was the end of the text that concerned her most. He wanted to see her and buy her dinner, but desperately needed to borrow five thousand pounds to extend his visa. It would only be until his wealthy father visited him for Christmas. Stefan, being a true gentleman, offered to repay Dilys the generous sum of six thousand pounds. He remarked that, it was the very least he could do as compensation for her trust in him.

She texted back to say that she would certainly need some time to think about it. It was pretty much all she had in her life savings account at the Post Office but gaining that extra thousand pounds was very tempting. It meant two additional trips to Ireland, and she thought of the happiness that, could bring as she eventually neared retirement. Her mother always told her 'to sleep on things' but after two restless nights, she made her decision. The money was very efficiently transferred by the Post Office to Stefan's London bank account.

Three days later, she happily glimpsed his text while she was cleaning a particularly filthy bathroom in Hammersmith. She sat down wearily on the edge of the large tub and read every beautiful spelling mistake with heady joy. Stefan had successfully extended his visa and he invited her to have dinner with him at Claridge's Hotel that very evening. She felt quite overwhelmed at the very thought of such a romantic setting. On her way home, she stopped suddenly on a whim at a reputable charity shop window to stare longingly at a beautiful red dress reduced in their sale. It was the sort of elegant dress one saw being worn by ladies in the Farm Street Church and community, and she gasped at being able to afford the sixty-five-pound price tag. It fitted her to perfection, and she joyfully told the assistant that, she planned to wear her mother's old pearl necklace with the dress. She nodded and smiled faintly at Dilys.

She raced into the bathroom and slyly borrowed a little of Shakira's expensive bath oil from Harrods. This late afternoon soak was a very rare luxury, and she allowed her mind to drift as a shroud of steam enveloped her tired, lily-white body. It truly felt as if the very handsome Stefan had tiptoed into her empty, lonely London life. It was nothing short of a miracle.

Dilys walked with a confident air into Claridge's and being called 'Madam' by the courteous doorman, added unexpectedly to the sheer joy of the experience. She stood in the grand, yet understated entrance foyer and made a few subtle adjustments to her blue silk scarf and gleaming pearl necklace. The sheer elegance of the hotel and the inviting citrus smell of fresh flowers encouraged her to sit on one of the stylish sofas. Her regular Church readings had given her poise and inner confidence, so sitting alone to gather her thoughts in Claridge's was not remotely as frightening as Dilys had first envisaged.

After a delightful, but totally unexpected conversation with a very polite staff member who happened to come from Ballyhooley, a village she already knew well, she began to feel that this was the life to which she truly belonged. Dilys used to visit Ballyhooley village as a child when her mother called in to see her Uncle Eddie who made wooden hurlies in his garden shed. *The girl at Claridge's*, she thought, *was much too young to have even heard of her Uncle Eddie*. "A nice man, but a useless drunk!" her mother used to repeat on the bus home. Then, she always blessed herself and asked for God's forgiveness.

The girl showed her the way to the bar and suggested that Dilys may enjoy a cocktail while waiting for her husband.

"Thanks so much," said Dilys and was slightly embarrassed to have slipped into her Farm Street accent so easily. A handsome young man in a stiff white jacket escorted her gently to a table and handed her the cocktail list. Her name was taken, and a second cocktail list was placed on the opposite side of the table. The sheer array of cocktails was amazing to read, but the prices shocked her. I could shop for one week's groceries for the price of one of the drinks she thought and gulped a little when she saw the waiter return with a smile.

She pointed to the top of a page and said, "A glass of House Champagne would be perfect while I wait for my husband. Thank you so much." She was indeed surprised when the waiter asked her to try the Champagne.

"Delicious. Thanks so much."

"Certainly, Madam," and he bent over slightly while expertly pouring the energetic Champagne. "Are you dining with us Mrs Montague-Murphy?"

"Yes. Once my husband arrives, we will be having dinner," and she glanced nervously at her tiny wristwatch. "He's running rather late; another one of those horrid business meetings."

Dilys sipped the perfectly chilled Champagne very slowly and began to take in her sumptuous surroundings and the array of well-dressed guests. She smiled with a certain satisfaction at being called 'Mrs Montague-Murphy' and then remembered that she was not even wearing a wedding ring. The Champagne helped her to relax, and she worried less about having to explain her young husband. She sat quite demurely in a sea of strangers knowing that Stefan, already an hour late, would soon walk in to warmly greet her. After all, Claridge's was his idea. *He may even bring me flowers,* she thought and smiled broadly at a work of art on the wall by her table. At that moment, the waiter returned, and she ordered another glass of champagne.

Dilys entered the restaurant feeling slightly tipsy, but it was just as if she was climbing those steps in the Church to deliver one of her solemn readings. She had ignored the subdued ping of the text a few minutes earlier while she lightly sprayed her neck from a selection of colognes in the very refined ladies' washroom.

She loved the intimacy and lighting of the restaurant and the space between the tables offered the luxury of privacy.

Dilys examined her roughened hands carefully. The smell of the exotic lavender and avocado moisturiser energised her senses. A few hours earlier, those same hands were cleaning shit from a stained toilet bowl in Hammersmith. She silently toasted herself with a glass of Chablis, kindly recommended by the wine waiter. "From skivvy to Lady, and all in one day! Thank you, Stefan."

She stared at the empty chair opposite, but no longer had any feelings of regret. Claridge's Hotel was teaching her something new and very potent about life, and she would nurture these memories in the coming lonely years.

The waiter seemed a little perplexed when Dilys insisted on paying her bill in cash. She took a lingering pleasure in removing the large wad of notes from her handbag. She counted them very carefully and added an extra twenty-pound note for the waiter. She stopped him suddenly from removing the pile of cash and dipped back into her handbag and added the defaced fiver to the plate.

Before shutting the shiny harps, she hurriedly read Stefan's text. He had been mugged at Victoria Station and all five thousand pounds stolen. Dilys smiled sadly and picked up her unfinished glass of wine. She silently toasted the very mean, but wealthy widow, Mrs Maggie Crump in Hammersmith, whose money she had stolen that morning from a rusty old commercial soap tin hidden in her filthy bathroom.

The polite doorman at Claridge's opened the taxi door for her. It was already gone midnight, but Mrs Montague-Murphy was returning a little unsteadily to her rented room at Shakira's modest terraced house a changed woman.

111

The Dance Band

Kitty Crowley sat in front of an oval shaped mirror in her untidy bedroom and tied her red hair into an uncannily neat bun. Her pale face was unblemished, and she had large, lively, trusting green eyes. The warm July sunshine penetrated the dark space like an old cinema projector and every movement of her nimble hands caused particles of dust to form erratic patterns like fireflies in the stuffy afternoon air. Her bedroom window was rarely opened, and the smells emanating from her make-up suitcase were enough to choke any family member who dared to enter Kitty's coveted, private space.

Usually, once a year, her mother Mary did a good spring clean of the small farmhouse and forced the loft bedroom window open while gasping for breath. She was asthmatic, and the combined smells of stale body odour and mascara made her gasp, while she struggled with the rusty window catch. Every April, her son Brendan promised faithfully to repair the latch, but it was soon forgotten in the mayhem of Irish family life on a medium sized farm.

Brendan, a strapping lad of twenty-one, was one year older than Kitty. Mary experienced a very difficult birth with Kitty, so no more children were possible. For that, she was seen as a flawed woman by her often brutal and ill tempered, older husband. Some of the villagers had also taken a dislike to her lack of fertility. Dan was fast approaching sixty and was mentally preparing to hand over the farm to Brendan. However, he kept making excuses and told Mary that, once their only son reached a quarter of a century, the farm would most likely be his. It was the 'most likely' bit that, always worried her. Mary knelt and prayed nightly, that Brendan would find a nice local girl from good farming stock. She thought that he already had an eye for Kitty's best friend, Maureen O' Hara, but she was regarded as most unsuitable. Maureen was maybe twenty-six or seven, wore far too much make-up, and she worked in the only grocer's shop in Rathmullen. Both Maureen and her mother Maisie were partial to a drop of whisky it was told.

"She will not cross this threshold as a bride! Over my dead body," shouted Dan one evening when Kitty mentioned her best friend's attraction for Brendan.

"Sure, I suppose she's a wee bit too old for our boy," her mother remarked quietly towards the glowing hearth, with a worried frown.

The girls were bosom buddies and their weekly Sunday ritual in summer was to go dancing at the open-air stage in Rathmullen. The stage was positioned in thick woodland and on the open field side, it commanded an enviable view of the Galtee mountain range. Often, these rugged peaks were shrouded in cloud and mist, even in the height of summer. It was the summer of 1967, and the local people were beginning to doubt if these dance stages would actually survive. The gradual arrival of television in Rathmullen meant, that young people were beginning to form an addiction for the flickering black and white screens. The Murphy family didn't own one on the grounds of cost. Dan was adamant that they should wait until the price dropped and rental was not an option for him either.

At one point, he contemplated selling old Bessy, one of his prize milking cows to buy a television set. On the morning of the sale, when the truck drew into the farmyard and Dan entered the barn with a rope halter, the forlorn look in Bessy's great big eyes caused him to stop in his tracks. He stroked old Bessy in his normal way and hid the dangling rope behind his back.

"Your home is here, old Bessy, and always will be," and with a tear glistening in Dan's right eye, he shut the barn door firmly.

"That Dan Crowley has gone pure mental," said the truck driver to his young mate as they reversed skilfully out of the small farmyard. So, no television would reach the farmhouse until the cold winter of 1970.

Kitty always helped her mother to do the wash up after the Sunday dinner while her father and Brendan relaxed by the fire. Turf blazed in the hearth all through the year to enable to back boiler to heat valuable water for the household. A small bathroom had been installed during the previous summer, and this was considered a real touch of luxury at the time. The Crowleys were renowned for their cleanliness and Dan joked, that Brendan took more baths than any Irish 'Nancy Boy.'

Kitty's make-up ritual usually started about 3 p.m. and she devoted three hours to this operation. She had taken a fancy to at least four members of the 'eight men' dance band. They had no name, just simply 'The Dance Band.'

They were all local lads from the village, and two of the members were well into their sixties. Dan went to school with Jack Foley, who played the violin: such a majestic instrument, but certainly not in the trembling hands of Jack Foley.

"That man couldn't read a newspaper, never mind a sheet of music," Dan often joked with Brendan. "And as for that clown Lungs O' Leary, he hasn't a musical note in his thick skull. Screaming into a microphone like a constipated banshee. Holy Jesus, where did his poor parents find the likes of him for a son!"

Kitty would always defend every member of the dance band with fierce loyalty and hated to hear her father say such things. She had quite a temper on her, and no one could joke about the young guitar player called John McNamara. He was by far the most handsome young man in the band. Kitty waltzed slowly past the band every Sunday evening with her eyes firmly fixed on John in his dark suit and pretty black tie. Their ties were fixed under the collars of their white, starched shirts and the neat upside-down, V-shape captivated young Kitty. She almost swooned at the rugged beauty of John McNamara; whose face had a deep country tan from working in the fields in all weathers. It troubled Kitty, that she also had eyes for Larry Doherty on the maracas. There was Lungs O' Leary on the accordion; then that Michael Magner, with the wide, innocent smile, who always played the banjo and violin so sweetly. She met each of their eyes in a trance when she stumbled past, usually in the arms of an older villager smelling strongly of porter, vanilla pipe smoke and stale sweat.

She normally hung about with Maureen, waiting patiently for the band to pack up their instruments and leave the rickety, makeshift stage. The romantic, lingering looks she saw portrayed in the cinema in Fermoy never seemed to materialise. The girls blamed it on the dance band feeling exhausted after over two hours of constant dance music.

"Your brother, Brendan, is the best-looking young man in the county, and he rarely comes here," said a sad-faced Maureen late one Sunday evening while the stage was closing down. Kitty got a fit of the giggles, remembering what her parents had said.

"He's not really interested in girls," remarked Kitty with a sigh. "But sure, he's still young," she added and picked up her handbag. She sniffed the material and told Maureen that, the paraffin and crystals used on the stage had stained it badly. Both girls linked arms and walked through the growing darkness on the tree track leading in the direction of the village.

"Sure, I badly need a husband," said Maureen wistfully when they parted company by Barry's Pub in the centre of the village. Kitty giggled and picked up her old bicycle before heading off on the uphill journey home. She whistled gently and smiled as the late evening breeze tickled her face and ruffled her flowing, freshly washed hair. Her thoughts drifted back longingly to John McNamara. The narrow saddle between her strong buttocks masked an unexpected wetness through the front of her flimsy white knickers.

The snow fell heavily on Christmas Eve morning and by noon, the Galtee Mountains stood like giant, freshly iced Christmas cakes on the sunny horizon. Dan stood by the cowshed and patted Brendan on his broad shoulders. Mary witnessed this rare show of affection and smiled while she quietly closed the half door to the kitchen. She went to the table to begin making potato and onion stuffing for the goose. Instinct told her that Brendan would get the farm as a Christmas present, despite their being still no hint of romance in his young life.

A fat looking goose was delivered as the afternoon surrendered the clear, but weak sunlight to winter gloom. Maureen O' Hara propped a heavy bicycle by the cowshed and struggled to remove the freshly plucked bird from the front carrier.

"May God have mercy on us, Maureen. Whatever caused them to send you out in this dangerous weather? Surely that Daly lad could have delivered our goose this morning. Come in, come in, girl and have a cup of tea," and Mary stepped back indicating a spot on the crowded kitchen table for the goose.

Kitty raced down the narrow, rickety stairs from her loft bedroom and both girls embraced by the roaring turf fire. Steam was already rising from the melting snow on Maureen's green oilskin jacket. Her mittens looked a forlorn pile of soggy wool by the hearth. The warm farmhouse kitchen was festooned with clusters of red, berried holly, and a lighted crib glowed on top of the family's robust Bush radio. Kitty helped Maureen to dry her hair and soon her complexion glowed from the icy weather and the exertion of the steep cycle, much of it uphill in the snow.

"Sure, it was such a lovely cycle out here in the sunshine. It's no problem for me, Mrs Crowley and I have a good front light for the journey back," before gladly

117

accepting a cup of scalding, strong tea and a slice of Christmas cake at the table.

"I mustn't linger, Mrs Crowley. The weather is set to turn nasty about five and Father Corbett is even thinking of cancelling midnight Mass. The last one was cancelled, I am told, back on Christmas Eve 1959," and she sipped the hot tea and smacked her shiny red painted lips. "It's a smashing cup of tea. Mrs Crowley. Happy Christmas to all of you."

Some very interesting facts were revealed about the Dance Band members when the Crowley family and Maureen settled in front of the warm turf fire on Christmas Eve evening. Mary had served a generous supper of rashers, black pudding, eggs and fried potatoes, washed down with two large pots of tea. The atmosphere was strained by Maureen's unexpected presence, but the forecast was accurate, and snow fell heavily across the silent countryside. Mary insisted that, Maureen was to share a bed with Kitty. When Kitty joked lightly that, Maureen would much prefer sharing with Brendan, her father exploded in anger.

The tumblers of whisky were re-filled and soon the atmosphere was relaxed and jolly; even Dan had a twinkle in his eye.

"Sure, 'tis strange all the same," and Dan downed his third measure of whisky with relish. "I'll have the same again Mary, sure it's Christmas Eve in old Ireland," and put his tumbler by the hearth. The flames from the turf fire caused the crystal glass to cascade coloured rays of light across the stone floor. "None of the lads in that band show any signs of marrying. That can't be right Maureen, can it?"

Kitty sat next to a red-faced Maureen on what used to be the back seat of an old Morris Minor, which belonged to

Dan's Aunt Evelyn. She had given the car to Dan; that had been her pride and joy, before she set sail for a new life in New York. The big city was to claim her, and she never set foot on Irish soil again.

Brendan drank a second whisky and kept casting glances in the gloom at Maureen. Mary noticed such things, and she busied herself making generous ham sandwiches. The onion and fresh thyme aroma of the goose stuffing gave the air a real festive pungency.

"They are not the marrying kind I suppose," said a sad faced Maureen. "A few good lookers in the band but looks don't always make for a happy marriage. Do they, Mrs Crowley?"

Mary looked up from cutting thick slices of crusty bread.

"Don't go asking me, Maureen O' Hara, for God's sake. Sure, I captured a handsome man, and look at my fine son, Brendan, over there." She finished her task of making a big plate of freshly boiled ham sandwiches, which were passed around the fireplace. They all ate in comfortable silence. Dan went on chewing, and truly appreciating the thick crusts. Then, Brendan downed his second whisky and went to pour more for himself and his father. He shyly raised his glass and said,

"Merry Christmas, Mam, Dad, Kitty and the lovely Maureen." He took a sip and coughed abruptly into the fireplace.

"Holy Jesus. That took my breath away. I've been thinking all summer, Dad. A bit like some members of the dance band you see. I'm not the marrying kind either. So, I may as well tell you all right now that, I'm setting sail for a new life in New York, early in the New Year."

119

There was a sickening silence, and Kitty, in a hunched position, watched the tears flowing freely down her mother's exhausted face. They sparkled like melting icicles in the firelight.